Walk Across The Sea

BOOKS BY SUSAN FLETCHER

Dragon's Milk

The Stuttgart Nanny Mafia

Flight of the Dragon Kyn

Sign of the Dove

Shadow Spinner

SUSAN FLETCHER

Walk Across The Sea

SCHOLASTIC INC.
New York Toronto London Auckland Sydney
Mexico City New Delhi Hong Kong Buenos Aires

No part of this publication may be reproduced in whole or in part, or stored in a retrieval system, or transmitted in any form or by any means, electronic, mechanical, photocopying, recording, or otherwise, without written permission of the publisher. For information regarding permission, write to Atheneum Books for Young Readers, Simon & Schuster Children's Publishing Division, 1230 Avenue of the Americas, New York, NY 10020.

ISBN 0-439-45796-3

12 11 10 9 8 7 6 5 4 3 2 1   2 3 4 5 6 7/0

Printed in the U.S.A.   40

First Scholastic printing, November 2002

Book design by Abelardo Martínez
The text of this book is set in Janson Text.

For the entire staff of the Lake Oswego Library,
with years of gratitude.

Contents

PARTING WATERS

To come to our home in the lighthouse, we had to walk across the bottom of the sea.

Sometimes I felt like Moses, when he parted the Red Sea to escape from Pharaoh's army. Excepting these waters didn't make a wall on either side, like in the Bible—just regular workaday waves. And there were no Egyptians or chariots anywhere about.

Still, there *was* a parting of waters. Twice a day, at ebb tide, the ocean rolled back to uncover a rocky isthmus between the mainland and our island. Sea bottom.

We had to pick our way midst boulders and heaps of driftwood, midst tide pools and gurgling streams. I'd lift my skirts to keep them dry, but there was nothing to be done about my shoes. So Papa bought me boots—tall, black, over-the-shoe boots made of India rubber.

I loved to peer at the sea creatures, so curious,

bared to light: starfish clutching like bright orange hands to the rocks, sea urchins bristling with purple spines, hermit crabs scrabbling about in their stolen seashell caps. Seemed like I was looking beyond the surfaces of things into a secret part of Creation, an enchanted place.

And to me, it *was* enchanted. It was paradise—for a while. Not just the walk across the seafloor, but everything about that place: the brown pelicans that sailed like schooners past our windows; the spouting whales; the lantern room at night, where the beacon sent slivers of rainbows shivering across my body, where I could close my eyes and *feel* the light as it passed, warming me all the way through.

You would have loved it there, Andrew John. I'm sorry you can't grow up there. It's my fault, but I don't regret it. Not for me. For *your* sake, though, I'm sorry.

1

*March 1886
Crescent City, California*

THE CHINA BOY

The beginning of the end of our life in the lighthouse was the day the goat got loose.

Well. There were many such days. Papa had bought her—Parthenia—to crop the poison oak and blackberry bushes that threatened to overtake our island. The milk was extra blessing.

Parthenia did her job too well. When she had taken her fill of brambles, she commenced upon Mama's vegetables and roses. Mama gave roses the go-by in time, but Papa built fence after fence for the garden before he finally set up one that goat looked upon as a discouragement.

After that, she raided other folks' gardens. She would escape the island at ebb tide, and afterward we would hear reports—Mrs. Somersby at church fuming about her hollyhocks, Horace Ahrens at school giving account of his mother's lost cabbages, Dr. Wilton from the hospital lamenting his late nasturtiums. Dr. Wilton was goodhearted about it though. He said Parthenia went tripping through the tiny clapboard hospital, entertaining the patients. The whole place felt jollier when she was there.

But Papa said it was not right to let Parthenia run loose. Besides, he said, the heathen Chinamen in the shanties at the edge of town were known to eat all manner of meat—rat meat, crow meat, cat meat, dog meat. They'd likely look upon Parthenia as a tasty supper indeed. Still, that cantankerous goat *would* escape. She could gnaw through any rope. She could jump atop her shed and vault across the fence. She could lean against the slats and knock them flat. If she purely wanted out, we couldn't hold her—just slow her down. It was my job to find her and fetch her home before the tide came in.

This day I'm telling of was a Saturday early in March—two years ago, when I was thirteen.

Parthenia had tucked into Mrs. Overmeyer's primroses, and that lady was none too pleased. "Eliza Jane McCully," she said when I came upon the scene, "you get that goat out of my garden, do you hear me? Shoo! Goat, shoo! Oh, my primroses! My poor, poor primroses!"

It took some doing to cultivate primroses so near the Pacific Ocean, with the constant salty wind and the sandy soil. Primroses—and other flowers—were a luxury and purely cherished by folks who grew them. I tied a rope around Parthenia's neck, and we played tug-o'-war for a spell, until she clapped eyes on the violets by the hospital and made a beeline in that direction. I managed to steer her away, toward the bluff above the isthmus. "Folks get contentious, with you laying into their flowers," I told her. "Haven't you noticed? Haven't you wondered why all the conniptions when you're about?"

Parthenia bleated mournfully, looked back at me with great, round, sorrowful eyes. She was misunderstood, she seemed to say. She was only *hungry*.

I first caught sight of Wah Chung when we reached the edge of the bluff. I didn't know yet he was called Wah Chung. I didn't know a blessed thing about him—save that he was squatting beside some rocks on the path to our island, his long pigtail hanging down his back beneath a wide, flat straw hat. A Chinaman. Seemed like he was writing something. Or drawing, maybe.

I stood there a tick, not knowing what to do. I was forbidden to mill about the China shanties, as some children did, buying litchi nuts and ginger candies. "Heathen things," Papa called them. So I stayed away. I was forbidden even to speak to a Chinaman. "If you see one coming toward you," Papa said, "step away and don't look at him. If you meet their eyes, they might try to converse with you. Best have nothing to do with them."

But the tide was on the uprise that afternoon. It had already swallowed up most of the isthmus, and the thin, foamy edges of waves washed across the narrow way that remained. I couldn't get home without passing quite near to this Chinaman. And I dared not wait for him to leave.

If it hadn't been for Parthenia, I might have turned back. The Wiltons let me stay with them whenever it was needful—when I became stranded on the mainland unexpectedly, or when, because of the tides, I had to leave for school early or turn homeward late. Mrs. Wilton had devised a signal to show that I was safely settled at their house: a yellow banner hung above their front porch and visible from the island. But the invitation did *not* include Parthenia. And besides, I didn't hanker for more doings with gardeners on a rampage.

I hurried along the steep path down the bluff. The brisk, sea-smelling wind whipped at my skirts and coat. It was a clear day, rare this time of year. High, thin clouds raced shoreward across a forever sky; gulls wheeled and cried overhead. Parthenia, at once seeming eager to be home, minced along before me, her udder bulging, flapping side to side. As we picked our way through the heaps of driftwood I saw the Chinaman glance toward us and away. He rose partway to his feet, seemed to think better of it, then squatted back on his heels and stared hard into the tide pool. It came to mind that he might wish to be shut of me as fervently as I wished to avoid him. But I had cut off his avenue of retreat.

Drawing near, I saw that he was holding a paintbrush and a sheet of paper tacked to a board. An ink jar sat on a rock beside him. A wave lapped over his bare feet and wet the legs of his baggy denim trousers, but he did not try to escape it by moving into our path. He sat like a stone. When we had nearly come abreast, Parthenia gave a quick, hard lurch in the Chinaman's direction and tried to bite his hat. I yanked her away and stepped sideways into a tide pool, flooding my boots with cold water, soaking my skirt and petticoat to my knees. A jet of anger spurted up inside me. This was *our* path to *our* island. What business had he here?

He did not look up. I cinched Parthenia's rope, clambered out of the pool and, shoes sloshing in my boots, marched for home.

But now Parthenia dawdled. She kept craning back to ogle the Chinaman, no doubt lusting after his hat. I slapped her flanks to urge her along—a mistake, I discovered. She balked— head down, ears back, legs splayed. "Come *along*, Parthenia," I said between clenched teeth. For pure cussedness that goat could not be beat. She backed toward the mainland, glaring at me. I jerked her rope sharp—another mistake. She wheeled round and bolted toward the Chinaman so quick, she took me off guard. Her rope slipped, burning, through my hand. I snatched at it, missed, and stumbled forward, hoping to catch hold of goat or rope before she reached the Chinaman.

He had turned to stare. His eyes looked wild. He leaped to his feet, flailed his arms, shouted something I couldn't understand. My heart stopped. Was he threatening me? Trying to scare me away from Parthenia so he could steal her? But something about the way he moved made me look over my shoulder, and then I saw it—a wave, a great, tall breaker, looming behind me. I ran, tripped, fell—my skirts were heavy, clinging. I got up and scrambled across a heap of rocks to a sturdy-looking boulder, then clung to the land-ward side as Papa had taught me—crouching, nestling into the curves of it, digging my fingers into its crannies. And the wave came roaring down upon me. Green water—not just white water and foam. It poured over my head, engulfed me to my waist, knocked me about, tried to jerk my feet from under me and pry me away. I pressed against the boulder until barnacles cut into my skin. The current dragged at me, so strong. My fingers slipped; I was peeling away. . . .

Then it was past. I dashed the stinging salt spray from my eyes and scanned the sea. Though water still sucked at my skirts below my knees, I saw nothing alarming on the horizon.

A sneaker wave. I had been caught by them

before, though never so direly as this, and Papa warned me constantly against them. *Never turn your back on the sea*, he always said—though of course we must, at times. But it was folly to do so for long.

And now I heard a piteous bleat. Parthenia! I turned to see her flailing in the arms of the Chinaman. I had a mind to shout at him, to tell him to put her *down*, but then I saw that he was wading toward me. "You . . . goat," he said. He set her down in the ebbing water and held out the end of the rope to me. He was drenched, head to foot. Hat gone, long blue jacket torn, a fresh gash across one cheek. He stood just my height, I saw. He seemed . . . my age, or very near.

A China *boy*.

Parthenia bleated again, long and deep and sad. She was a sorry sight, all stomach, bones, and udder, with her hair plastered to her body, and her slotted amber eyes reproaching me. All at once I felt ashamed. I had not given her a thought, had just run to save my own skin. And yet this China boy . . . Had he rescued Parthenia from the wave? Or just plucked her up after it had passed?

He held out the rope again. "You . . . goat," he said.

I glanced over my shoulder at the sea—all was well—then hastened toward the China boy. I kept my eyes averted. But at the last moment, when I was about to mumble my thanks, my eyes snagged on his—strange, lidless-seeming, almond-shaped. Something moved inside me, like a sudden shift in the wind.

The China boy ducked his head. I snatched the rope from his hand.

"Come along, Parthenia," I said sternly. *"Come along!"*

2

HEATHEN'S HAT

When I tell people I used to live in a lighthouse, most times they picture it wrong. They think of a tower with steps going round inside and just the lantern room on top. "Where did you sleep?" they ask me. "Where did you sup?"

But our lighthouse was truly a *house*. We had a spare bedroom downstairs, and a lean-to kitchen with a pantry you could walk into, and a fine sitting room with a pump organ and a banjo clock. Then up you went—round the spiral staircase— to two more bedrooms and a large storage cupboard. Nearly just like a house. It was only when you went upstairs *again* that it began to feel like a lighthouse.

Still, there were hints along the way. When you looked out the downstairs windows, you could see that the granite outer walls stood two feet thick. And the stairs were not like stairs in ordinary houses; they curved along the inside of a wide, brick-lined tube.

That was the tower. Up past the bedrooms it tapered inward. A few turns around and you came to the tiny service room, with its curved bench along one wall and its black iron floor. Then up again—scale a short ladder through a hole in the metal ceiling—to the lantern room.

The lens, on its iron platform, filled the room: hundreds of curved glass prisms all set together in a barrel shape, near the size of our cookstove. A narrow ring of floor surrounded it, and a cylinder of glass windows encircled all.

It was like standing in the midst of the sky.

From there, on clear days, you could see *everything:* the muddy streets and clapboard buildings of Crescent City; the long, thin wharf; the fishing boats anchored in the harbor; the rocky, timbered shoreline nigh on to Oregon; the coast south beyond the bay toward Eureka; the Saint George Lighthouse on its faraway reef; and miles and miles of sea.

"Papa," I said, on the morning after the sneaker wave, as I looked down on the slumbering town, "why did the Chinamen come here?"

This was my favorite time. Most mornings—when tides and school permitted—I would sleepily climb the stairs to the service room at dawn. "Good morning, Sunshine," Papa would say, smiling and handing me my apron. He said the same thing every time.

I put on the plain linen apron, took the feather brush from its peg, and climbed the ladder to the lantern room. Papa had stopped the clockwork that rotated the beacon; he had blown out the lamp. I nestled in the warmth that still pooled about the lens and began to dust.

It was an important job, caring for the lens. Lives depended on it. Papa had entrusted it to me bit by bit, and only after I had begged. When I was six, he had taught me how to dust it; when I was eight, he had shown me how to wipe it with the linen cloth; when I was ten, he had let me polish it with the buff skin. Now I did everything all by myself, even the tricksome work of wiping off oil spots with a cloth dipped in spirits of wine.

The lens was the heart of the lighthouse, Papa said, and must be cared for just so. He'd taught me to work carefully, without haste, like the sun easing up into the sky. "There is a right way, and there is a wrong way," he would always say. "What is wrong cannot be right."

Now, as I waited for an answer, teasing dust from the grooves between prisms, I watched Papa open the door in the lens and take out the heavy lamp for cleaning. The acrid smell of kerosene tickled my nose—familiar, comforting.

"Papa?" I asked again. "The Chinamen?"

An osprey dropped out of the sky, snatched up a fish in its talons. It labored skyward until the light of dawn, too new yet to touch earth, stained its wings pink.

"There is fighting in their country," Papa said at last, edging past with the lamp. "Chinaman against Chinaman. And famine always follows war. They have come for work and food."

"Then why do folks want them to leave?" I asked. "A body *needs* food."

I knew why the Chinese had been forced to leave Eureka last year. A Chinaman had shot and killed a white man. It was an accident, I knew—but Papa said that sort of thing couldn't be allowed. Still, nothing like that had happened here. Our Chinese seemed odd, but not murderous. Even when schoolboys threw stones at them, they only ducked and hurried away.

Papa stopped by the hole in the floor, turned to face me. "They're heathens, Eliza Jane. And they're taking the food out of good Christians' mouths."

"They don't believe in Jesus?" I asked as he started down the ladder.

"No," he said. "Nor even God. They're heathens, as I have told you before."

I knew that Chinamen were called heathens —everyone knew that. But I hadn't given much thought to what *heathen* meant. It was a thing folks said against Chinamen and Indians. A thing like *sinner*, only worse. But now . . . *Nor even God.* I couldn't fathom that—no God. Who would watch over you and protect you? Who would hear your prayers?

"What *do* they believe, then?" I asked down through the hole.

"Heathenish things. They have practices. . . . But best you know nothing of them. Guard the portals of your mind, Eliza Jane."

Finished with dusting, I sat down on the floor by the ladder, dangled my feet through the opening. I handed the feather brush down to

Papa, took the linen cloth he passed back, then watched as he scrubbed soot from the lamp's chimney with a squeaky, rubbing sound. He looked so handsome in his lightkeeper's uniform, with his dark, neatly trimmed beard. A thin white scar sliced lengthwise through his lower lip—a memento of the time he risked his own life to save sailors in a shipwreck.

"Are they *all* . . . evil, then?" I asked. "What if one of them did something good?"

Now I had edged onto the subject I wanted to discuss. For I had not yet told about the China boy who had saved Parthenia. The day before, when I had come in bloody and drenched and dirty, Mama had made such a to-do over my escape from the wave that I had scarce been able to put in a word. She had hugged me so tight I could feel the hardness of her belly, where the baby was. Then Papa had come in from the carpentry shop and, between his praise for my levelheadedness in clinging to the boulder and his chidings for my not having watched the sea, I had not known how to broach the subject of the China boy. Besides, I'd suspected that the chidings would crowd out the praisings if I told the whole story.

"All good comes from God," Papa said now. "There is no good where God is not embraced. And where there is no good, there is evil."

The China boy's hat washed up on the island later that day. It was only a mite tattered. Some of the straw had frayed and split, making it bulge in one spot, and a clump of kelp had knotted itself round the black tying cords.

I ought to have set the hat on the burning pile— buried it there so Parthenia wouldn't nose it out. But I wavered. Papa thought that Chinamen were evil, but this one had seemed . . . like a regular boy. I recollected how he had stood up, then squatted back down, as if he had not known what to do when I came onto the path. How he had skewed his gaze from me at first, as if he were as leery of me as I was of him. I recollected how, when he *had* looked, his eyes had seemed serious—but not unfriendly.

He had warned me of the wave. True, Parthenia might not have turned back if he hadn't been there, and then I would have seen the wave myself. But even so. If he hadn't waved his arms and shouted at me, the wave would have struck me without warning. Knocked me down, like as not. Carried me out to sea.

I untangled the kelp from the cords, tried to press out the bulge in the sodden straw.

Well. Even heathens needed hats.

When the tide ebbed that afternoon, I walked in to the mainland, scouted about for just the right boulder, set the hat atop it, and weighed it down with two heavy stones.

3

CONTRAPTION

The next day I was eager to check on that hat.

Well. I left for school before dawn because of the tides. The rocks that edged the island were too steep to permit a boat landing; every dock ever built there had soon been washed out to sea. So we lived by the tides. Ebb tide came twice a day and bared the isthmus for two to four hours, more or less. Papa had a little book with tables of a whole year's tides printed there inside. But we could reckon when it was safe to cross by whether the tide rocks—two good-sized boulders on the isthmus—stood above the waves. We *felt* the tides someway, how they edged along in time, each ebb later day by day until it crossed midnight and became early again. There were times I could hear the very moment when the tide changed: a sudden, strange silence and then a booming surge of waves that was somehow louder, somehow *surer,* than the ones just before.

Today I would cross near the end of an early-morning ebb and stay at the Wilton place until school began. The isthmus would open again not long after school let out. Other days, I stayed after school at their house, waiting to be able to cross. There were days when I arrived late to school or left early because of the tides. There were days when I couldn't go at all; Miss Argle-mile prepared my lessons ahead, and I worked on them at home.

Now Mama handed me a lantern, tucked my braids into my slicker, admonished me to watch the waves.

She would watch them, I knew. She used to walk me to shore every day, but now, with the baby coming, Papa wouldn't let her. Still, every time I turned back, I saw her—a lone, dark figure standing straight against the sky.

I hurried across the isthmus, listening hard to the rumble and hiss of the waves, turning back often to find the dim shapes of them. The beacon swept across the rough surface of the water—steady and reliable, a comforting sight. A chill wind plastered my skirts and slicker to my legs and spat out a fine, misty rain.

Though the sky was turning gray in the east, the light did not reach my feet. My lantern picked out the flat rocks and dry patches, the paths through the heaped driftwood near shore—all stitched over with silvery needles of rain.

When I came to the boulder where I had left the Chinaman's hat, I lifted my lantern to see.

Gone.

I raked the light slowly across the top of the boulder. The stones I had set there remained.

Could be the wind pried the hat loose.

Might be the China boy took it.

The porch lamp was lit for me at the Wilton place. While I tugged off my boots, Mrs. Wilton hung my coat and bonnet by the cookstove to dry, then bustled about to prepare me a cup of cocoa and a heap of griddle cakes. She stood watching me eat, her bosom resting easy on her folded arms, her face crinkled and soft as linen hung to dry in the sun.

"We missed you at church yesterday," she said. "I hope your mama's well."

She had enquired after Mama every day since last November—before even I had known the baby was coming.

I nodded. "Tolerable well, thank you. But she was feeling a mite weary."

Mrs. Wilton frowned. "Weary's to be expected, but more than that. . . . Keep a close eye on her now for us, won't you?"

"How's that mother of yours, Eliza?" I heard the doctor's hearty voice a moment before he appeared round the corner.

"Well, thank you," I said again.

He pulled up a chair, lowered himself into it with a soft grunt, combed a finger through his red-and-gray mustache. "Have you felt the baby yet? Has she let you?"

I nodded, blushing. Just last week Mama had patted her apron where her belly bulged out and said, "Set your hand here, Liza." When I hesitated, she said, "This is just between us girls. No need to tell Papa." She took my hand and put it there, on the bulge. I'd felt it then, breaking the surface of the curving hardness beneath my hand: a fluttering movement, like a butterfly under her skin. "Isn't that a wonder?" Mama had said. "Baby's kicking."

I had stood there, *listening* to the baby with my hand, imagining its tiny feet thrusting out against the borders of its world. Mama had watched me, smiling. "We've got a spirited one on our hands, Liza. You're a tad mettlesome, aren't you, sweetie?" she said, looking down at her belly.

Now Dr. Wilton harrumphed, tamped tobacco in the bowl of his pipe. "Tell your mother not to work so hard. She's a cultivated flower—needs tending. Tell her she should have someone in to help."

"She has Mary Connor in from town once a week, on washday. Mama says, more than that and Mary'd be underfoot."

"Well, you help her too, Eliza Jane. You need to go to school—that's important—but help your mother as much as you can. You hear?"

I nodded.

He gave me a quick smile, then heaved himself up from his chair and shuffled into his office. Through the open doorway I could see an odd metal *thing*, about the size of a table lamp, on the doctor's desk. "What's that?" I asked Mrs. Wilton when the doctor had shut the door.

"*That*," she said tartly, "is his new con*trap*tion. It cost twice as much as my best tea service, and he's infernally proud of it. I can scarce drag him away from it, even to eat, and you know he's fond of eating. Watch," she whispered, leaning down to me. "Guthrie!" she called. "Eliza is admiring that . . . microwhatsit of yours. Would you care to show it to her?"

Slap-bang, the door swung open. "You're hankering for a look at my new microscope, Eliza Jane?" Dr. Wilton asked. He didn't wait for an answer. "Well, don't dawdle, missy. Come in! Come in!"

Mrs. Wilton gave me a nod and a knowing look as Dr. Wilton shooed me into his office.

It was a peculiar-looking machine. There was a brass tube like a very small spyglass, which pointed down at a square platform, which was held up from the desk by a black metal base. Below the platform was a mirror.

Jabbing his pipe stem at the machine, Dr. Wilton explained in a confounding sort of way how the lens made things look bigger, and what scientific principles lay behind it, and why this machine was so far superior to the old one he kept at the hospital. I must have looked as fuddled as I felt, for he set down his pipe and slid a small, flat circle of glass onto the platform and peered down into the tube. The table lamp made a shiny spot on his head beneath thin strands of graying hair. With stubby, competent fingers he turned a small metal disc.

"There," he said. "You look."

At first I couldn't see anything at all. I tried closing one eye, but Dr. Wilton told me to keep both of them open. "Look *into* the lens," he said. "It will come clear."

In a moment I got the knack of it. There was a blurry, pinkish something, like a rash. "Turn the knob," Dr. Wilton said. All at once a field of many objects—smooth and round, like pearls— swam into view.

"Red blood cells!" Dr. Wilton said as if he had discovered the Holy Grail. "And a few white ones too. But the white ones look purple because of the dye. You—"

I looked up, fuddled again. Dr. Wilton frowned at me, then his face suddenly cleared. He turned round and plucked up a glass jar full of dirty-looking water from a shelf. With a rubber dropper he dripped some of the water onto a different circle of glass, then covered it with yet another. He replaced the glass circle on the platform with these.

"Look," he said.

This time it was even more curious. There were little, green, snakelike squiggles; and tiny crescent moons; and hexagons; and outlandish spidery things; and graceful, gauzy shapes that looked like flower buds.

"What's this?" I asked.

"It's seawater."

"Seawater!"

"Yes! When you look through the lens, you can see the tiny organisms that live there."

I looked again. Organisms. Living things.

"They're invisible without the lens," Dr. Wilton said. "But *with* it . . ." He snapped his fingers. "Before your very eyes!"

A secret world, I thought. Like the starfish and sea urchins laid bare by the tide. Like the baby in Mama's belly. "This is . . . wondrous," I said.

Dr. Wilton nodded, regarding me with keen blue eyes. "Yes," he said, kind of slow. "Wondrous, indeed."

Later, before I left for school, Mrs. Wilton thanked me for feigning interest in the doctor's new contraption. "But I *was* interested," I said.

She looked at me oddly. "Truly?"

"Yes!"

"Well, then—that's fine! The doctor is . . . a bit lonesome, I often think. It's seldom he has occasion to palaver with other doctors. And no one else is as taken with these con*trap*tions as he."

4

THE BLURTS

There was a ruckus in the school yard when I arrived that morning. Not just the usual sort, with Amos Tyler and Stephen Somersby fiddling some poor six-year-old out of the choicest morsels in his lunch pail; or Izzy O'Brien yanking Fanny Plunkett's sash; or one of the various hair pullings, name callings, or shoves that now and again plagued the school yard peace.

No, this was an out-and-out donnybrook between Amos and William Gartner, the timber foreman's son. They were rasseling about on the ground, grunting and throwing punches.

I spotted three mops of gingery hair among the children that fringed the brawl. The Gump clan. "What brought this on?" I asked, coming up beside Sadie. "They're like to kill each other." Sadie Gump, my best friend, was an authority on the goings-on in town.

"William's pa fired Amos's pa, up at the lumber camp. Hired two Chinamen to replace him."

William got in a good lick to Amos's belly. But Amos, a large, blocky boy with a squarish face and fists the size of flatirons, clocked him in the mouth and commenced a stream of blood.

"Ouch," I whispered, then turned back to Sadie. "I know they've got Chinamen at the mills. But I've never heard of a Chinese lumberjack."

"Well, now you have. Pa says they'll work longer and cheaper than regular jacks. Just like in the mills. Dirt cheap, Pa says."

"What about him? Is he fearful for *his* job?"

Sadie shrugged. "Amos's pa was drunk. That's why he was fired. But cheap Chinese labor ain't gonna help *us* none, Pa says. Uh-oh. Here she comes."

Miss Arglemile was marching down from the schoolhouse. She was near as old as the preacher and half Amos's size—but tougher than last week's biscuits. She reached out and grabbed Amos by one ear, twisted it, pulled him off of

William. She handed William a handkerchief for his cut lip, then herded them both up to the schoolhouse and rang the morning bell.

William's lip stopped bleeding partway through the spelling lesson. Miss Arglemile had him rinse out her handkerchief under the pump and set it on the stove to dry. Then she made him stand in the back of the room, catercorner to where Amos had stood all morning. She let them out to lunch, though, one at a time. Afterward they were back in their seats.

And that might have been the end of it—with me having no part in it at all—excepting I got the blurts.

I have gotten the blurts for as long as I can remember, and they've caused me a world of trouble. Foot-in-mouth disease, Mama calls it. First time I can recall, I was five years old and witnessed Mrs. Somersby downing her third bowl of blackberry crumble at the church picnic. I traipsed right up to her and said, "No *wonder* you're so fat." You never saw a child hushed so quick.

"But it's true," I said later to Mama.

"Just because a thing's true is no call to say it," she told me. "A lady must learn to hold her tongue."

But truth is a powerful thing. Sometimes it purely cries out to be told.

I think Miss Arglemile was using the brawl as an excuse to teach us something, because later that day she turned the big globe so that China was facing out. She told us about the Celestial Empire, another name for China. Then she pointed out Kwangtung Province and the Pearl River delta. "This is where most of the Celestials in our community hail from," she said. "Can anyone tell why they came?"

I raised my hand, but Fanny was quicker on the draw. "The gold rush," she said. "They wanted to get rich."

"That's partly true. Before that, the Chinese built the road from Altaville to the Smith River valley and worked in the canneries. Then, in the fifties and sixties, many people—whites and Chinese—came to or through Crescent City looking for gold. But now the gold is gone and the Celestials are still coming to our land. Who can tell me why? Eliza?"

I was going to say what Papa had told me—about the fighting in their country, about the famine—when Amos butted in.

"To steal white folks' jobs," he said, looking

daggers at William. "They're thieves. Nothin' but thieves."

There was a red blotch on his cheek where the pie he had stolen from Derek Overmeyer's lunch pail had stained his face on the way in.

"*You're* a fine one to talk about thieves," I said. Blurted, more like. Amos leaped to his feet and started for me, but Miss Arglemile's voice, like a whip crack, stopped him.

"Amos!" Then she turned to me. "Eliza, we've spoken of this before. Both of you—see me after school."

Sadie waited outside until I had finished mopping the schoolhouse floor. At least I hadn't had to scrub the privy, like Amos. He'd jostled me—hard—when he thought Miss Arglemile wasn't looking. Turned out she had eyes in the back of her head.

I'd told Sadie about the China boy at lunch; now she wanted to walk past the shanties so I could point him out.

"No," I said. "Papa doesn't want me to talk to any Chinamen or have a blessed thing to do with them. You know that."

"We won't talk to him or nothin'. Just look. Ain't no harm in it."

"If Papa found out I was at the shanties . . ."

Sadie frowned, scratched her freckled nose. "Can't you just say I had an errand there? Come to think on it, I just might have one. I need you for protection. I'm scared."

"You?" I snorted. "Scared? Who'd believe that?"

"Well, don't you want to know if that China boy got his hat?"

I sighed. Once Sadie fixed her mind on a thing, it was nigh hopeless to argue her out of it. Besides, I *would* like to know about that hat.

Walking through town was a perilous proposition if you aimed to keep tolerable clean. In winter, fall, and spring the streets churned with muck. Summers, they billowed with dust. Lower Second Street, nearest the seashore, was perpetually mired in sand, and during specially fierce storms the waves broke right up onto First Street, leaving great stacks of logs at the very doors of the business houses.

Crescent City was a tired town when we came here, from Ohio, when I was three years old. By then the easy gold was gone. Some Chinamen had stayed, worked the last of the streams and diggings. But pickings were too slim for white folks, so hordes of them had pulled up stakes.

I could recollect when near a third of the buildings in town were empty clapboard shells. Kind of droopy and sad. But things were changing now.

Times were booming again, on account of timber. Steamers loaded with boards left the dock at least twice a week. There were two big mills near town, and talk of building a third. New folks had moved here—to feed and outfit the lumbermen, to transport timber and supplies. Folks had patched the abandoned buildings, perked them up with fresh paint, and were starting to put up more.

"Have you ever seen this China boy before?" Sadie asked me now.

We had stopped at the corner by the livery shop, waiting for the dray cart to pass. Mr. Hinkley drove his team at a strapping pace and thought nothing of splattering a body head to toe with mud.

"Can't say for certain." I'd seen a couple of China boys our age but never looked hard enough to tell one from the other.

We crossed Third Street, skirting the potholes, and clomped onto the wood-plank walk in front of the butcher shop. "It's peculiar he was setting right there by your island," Sadie said. "Seems like he'd know better—like he'd know your pa don't want them coming so near."

I shrugged. Another thing Papa wouldn't want was me going to look for the boy.

The China shanties stood on Second Street, near H Street. They were small and rickety, molting great, long flakes of paint. *Slovenly*, I'd heard Papa say. *A disgrace.* As we turned the corner the smell of them filled my nose: cooking smells, garbage smells, alien sweet-and-sour smells I could not identify. We walked by two Chinese women—one old, one young—wearing loose jackets and trousers, conversing in shrill, singsongy voices. One of them looked back as we passed. Were they talking about *us*? We shrank against the wall to make way for a burly China-man wearing a yoke on his shoulders, with buck-ets of water dangling from either end. Two more Chinamen passed, one near young enough to have been my China boy. I stole a quick, search-ing glance at his face.

"Was that him?" Sadie asked.

"No." This one's face was wider, someway, than I recollected. Not *him*.

Until a year ago this walk had teemed with folks—Chinamen in high-buttoned jackets and baggy trousers, wearing straw China hats or skullcaps or broad-brimmed hats of black felt. Chinese women, too, though not near so many. And white folks here aplenty: schoolchildren buying sugarcane and candy, lumbermen dropping off laundry at the washhouse, ladies shopping for spices and tea.

But Eureka changed all that. After the shooting the folks of that town had rounded up their Celestials and put them on ships bound for San Francisco. Ever since, there had been talk in this town of being shut of *our* Celestials. Some folks were refusing to buy from Chinese businesses, urging others to do the same. *Starve them out*, I'd heard Mr. Cuthbertson say. Many Chinese *had* moved away—near a hundred, I'd heard tell. Looked to me now like there couldn't be half that many left—though none of their shops had closed.

Sadie and I poked our heads inside the little general store. It was tidier than I'd expected: burlap bags full of rice and flour, barrels of sugar and tea, shelves stocked with strange-looking bottles and tins. I counted five Chinamen inside. But no China boy.

We peered into another shop—the herbalist's, Sadie said. Along the walls stood shelves lined, neat as a pin, with odd-shaped ceramic jars. Two Chinamen sat at a small wooden table, playing some sort of a game, I guessed. The men looked ancient—their faces like crumpled paper, their mustaches long and gray. The thin, stooped one, gesticulating at some tiles on the table, seemed to be scolding the short, round one, who smiled serenely and blinked like a cat. The thin one caught sight of Sadie and me, ceased with his scolding, started to creak to his feet. "Nothing today!" Sadie sang out, then tugged me along.

When we came to the washhouse, Sadie wanted me to go in. "No!" I said. "Papa would—"

"Then you wait here. I'll be back directly."

"Sadie—"

Before I could stop her, she opened the door and ducked inside.

I could hear talking, and a voice answering back. That Sadie! Leaving me here alone! What if someone saw me and told Papa? I leaned against the jamb, peeked through the half-open doorway. There was a clean, sharp smell of bleach and lye, and another smell, something smoky and sweet. The room was dim and bare, save for a rough-hewn wooden counter and a small porcelain sculpture of a fat, jolly man. Poking out of his head were two sticks— incense—and smoke drifted up from them. *Heathen practices.*

A man stood behind the counter—a smiling Chinaman in a skullcap, whose age I could not fix. Sadie, in her patched, raggedy frock, was chatting with him as if she knew him. She said something, and the Chinaman laughed. A friendly-sounding laugh.

Sadie knows Chinamen, I said to myself. Well. I had known that she did. Living here in town, she knew far more folks than I. They crossed paths. Grew . . . familiar. One of her brothers sometimes played with a little Chinese boy, and her uncle worked with Chinamen, down to the mill.

Still . . .

I wondered how it would be, to know a Chinaman.

Something bumped into my legs. I whirled round, stifling a scream. A glossy-haired Chinese child bounced off me, sat down hard on the walk, and began to howl. A Chinese woman appeared in the next doorway. She scooped up the child, with a wary look at me, and vanished inside.

"Guess what I found out?" Sadie stood beside me.

"What?"

"There's a new China boy in town, come from Oregon so's he could be with his grandpa. That skinny old man—the herbalist. That's him. This boy rode in with them Chinaman lumber-jacks. Fong says your China boy is likely *him*."

"Did . . . Fong . . . say anything about the hat?"

"Nope. Fong says he don't keep track of folks' hats. He—"

"Eliza!"

I turned to see Mrs. Wilton just outside the herbalist's door.

"Oh, and Sadie. How are you girls this after-noon?"

I gulped. "Well, thank you. We were just—"

"I had an errand and I made Eliza come," Sadie broke in. "How do, Mrs. Wilton?"

"Well indeed, thank you." My gaze was drawn to something she was carrying, a small parcel wrapped in Chinese paper. She must have seen me look, because she added, "Just a little something for my . . . constitution."

Her constitution? "But . . . can't the doctor fix it?"

Soon as I said it, I felt my face go hot. Oh, mercy. The blurts again.

But Mrs. Wilton only laughed. "He takes it too, dear. Tastes mighty good, and it's more efficacious than prunes."

5

SOMEONE'S SISTER

I couldn't help looking when I passed that boulder, going home. This morning it had been so dark.

The hat *was* gone, of course. But there was something else, something that glinted from a hollow atop the big rock.

A bottle. A bright blue bottle, no taller than my forefinger.

My heart jumped, got stuck at the base of my throat. "Wind didn't set *that* there," I murmured.

I picked it up, turned it over in my hands. Empty. There was a raised pattern on it, something that looked like the strange writing I'd seen on a small cloth sack of litchi nuts Horace Ahrens once brought to school.

Chinese litchi nuts.

Oh, mercy.

Could it be?

Might that China boy have left it here . . . for *me?*

Maybe it was here all along, and I just didn't see. Maybe it had been here for years.

Maybe.

Likely *not*.

I held it up to the feeble light that seeped through heavy clouds. It was the bluest blue, like looking down into a deep ocean pool on a summer's day.

But Papa wouldn't let me keep it. I knew that without asking. *Shun all heathenish things*, he had told me.

Still, it was just an empty bottle. It *would* make a dear vase with a clover blossom in it. Or I could keep it with my other treasures— sea-polished agates and shells.

I slipped it into my slicker pocket.

Forbidden fruit. The words popped into my mind as if Papa were here to say them. *Just like Eve.*

Well. No harm in keeping it, just for now. I *could* turn it over to Papa. I just might.

Later I would decide.

When I opened the front door, I heard giggles in the sitting room, so I knew Mrs. Pemberton had come calling. Mrs. Pemberton was the only soul I ever heard Mama giggle with. Laugh—that she would, at a seagull's antics, or when I told of some comical incident at school. But giggle—no. Except with Mrs. Pemberton. When those two ladies got together, away from menfolk and everyone else but me, I could see past Mama's careworn, grown-up face to the girl she had once been.

Mrs. Pemberton had brought her new baby, Martha Alice. I stared at the baby long after I had made my greetings—at the reddish blond fuzz on her head; at her wide, astonished eyes; at her ears, small as limpet shells, yet complicated as the chambers of a conch.

Mrs. Pemberton held out the baby to me, a soft, bunting-swaddled bundle. "Would you like to hold her?" she asked.

"Oh, yes!"

"Yes what, Liza?" Mama was giving me her *look*.

"Yes, please."

Mama was a stickler for manners. She grew up in Kentucky, "where ladies are *ladies*," she told me often enough for me to tire of hearing it. Same way with proper grammar. She'd let some lapses by—California quirks, she called them— but never an *ain't* or a double negative would pass my lips without a raised eyebrow or firm rebuke. She'd drummed them clean out of me.

Now I settled myself in a chair. Mrs. Pemberton gently laid the baby in my arms. I snuggled her close, careful to support her head and neck, as Mama showed me. Martha Alice did not feel much heavier than a doll—and yet she was so wondrously *alive*. Sentiments washed in waves across her plump, rosy face: surprise, cogitation, puzzlement, glee. At once, for no cause I could fathom, she thrust up her hands, waved them about, and cooed. I bent down, nuzzled her hair; she smelled like warm milk. She took hold of one of my braids and yanked it *hard*. "Ouch!" I laughed, along with Mama and Mrs. Pemberton. Gently I unclasped Martha Alice's fingers. Her nails were pink as cherry blossom petals and tiny as the wings of a fly.

"Eliza Jane will make a fine older sister," Mrs. Pemberton said.

Sister. I longed to be someone's sister. Sadie was sister to a whole entire tribe of siblings; all I wanted was one. A boy was what Papa prayed for—had done so for years. "Well, you never know," Mama said sometimes. "We had a girl before, and look how well she turned out." But I prayed along with Papa for a robust baby boy. We would go larking about together—that's what Mama called it. I would take him down to the flat boulder at the windward edge of the island, and we would watch the harbor seals at play on the shoals. I would teach him not to be afraid when gray whales swam in close to scrape off their barnacles on the rocks. We would feed the seagulls together, and hunt for agates, and explore the tide pools. On stormy nights I would take him up to the keeper's walk, to revel in the boom and hiss and rumble of the sea.

When he was older, he could help me with my chores. Maybe he could tend to Parthenia.

Of a sudden, Martha Alice kicked; her fists shot out. She wrinkled up her eyes and began to squall. I looked up in alarm. Mrs. Pemberton smiled, then took the baby from me. "There, now," she said softly. "There, now." Martha Alice whimpered, belched, sucked in a juddering breath, then seemed to melt into Mrs. Pemberton.

"Well!" Mama said. "There's gingerbread in

the pantry, Liza. You've yet a little time for larking about, and your chores are still awaiting."

At supper Papa astounded me by asking if I could keep the light alone, night after this. He had something to do on the mainland and would overnight at the Wiltons' because of the tides.

I had done all there was to do with the beacon, but never alone. Twice I had stayed up to help Mama keep the light when Papa was out at shipwrecks. This time Mama needed her rest. "She'll help if need be," Papa said. "But I'm certain you can tend it alone."

So I was all puffed up with pride, unready for the next thing he said: "Have you ever seen a Chinaman near the isthmus? A China boy?"

I gaped at him, scrabbling about in my mind to fix on what to say.

"Don't be alarmed, Eliza. I saw him yesterday, prowling about, but the problem will be put to rest soon enough. After this next meeting we'll know what to do."

"This . . . meeting?"

"The one I'll attend on the morrow. We'll resolve then—once and for all—what's to be done about the Celestials."

6

THE BABY

Sometimes, at sunset, when the wind stilled and the waters lay smooth, I used to gaze across the sky and imagine God was there. When clouds gathered on the horizon, deep purple and salmony pink, I would wait for a gap in them, an opening to what lay Beyond.

And sometimes it would happen: the clouds would part for a moment, and a burning gold light would come pouring across the sea—so powerful, so beautiful, it would flood me up with gratefulness that I'd been allowed to see it.

The sky was like that the night I tended the beacon alone. I felt a stillness inside me as I scraped the wooden match across the sandpaper, as flame bloomed up from the wick of the lamp, as I set on the cool glass chimney, shut the lens door, and pulled the lever for the clockwork to turn. I breathed in the clean, familiar smells of sulfur and kerosene and brass polish. It felt like a ritual, like church. *To give light to them that sit in darkness.* I wrapped myself in a blanket and stood watch as stars struck sparks in the dusk.

Of a calm night there was not much labor to lightkeeping. Every four hours the wick must be trimmed and the lamp refilled. The clockwork ran eight hours at a stretch; we rewound it when we trimmed the wick.

So Papa seldom stayed all night in the tower. He slept light and woke often, noting the beacon from time to time as it passed the bedroom window. It was only on stormy nights, when the vents in the tower room wall must be set time and again, that he never saw his own bed.

Those plaguey vents! You must let in just enough air for the flame to breathe, but a jot too much would snuff it. In the gusts and shifts of a stormy wind, you everlastingly fiddled with the vents. I wasn't as attuned as Papa to the rhythms of the wind, nor as adept at setting the vents, nor as dependable at waking on cue. I would stay in the tower all night.

Well. I had *thought* to do so.

It began such a peaceful night! I bided in the lantern room until well past dark—soaking in the warmth as the bull's-eyes passed, watching tiny rainbows go trembling across the windowpanes, listening to the well-oiled rumble of the clock-work. From there, standing with my back to the lens and looking out, I could see many shafts of light at once. Like the spokes of a great wagon wheel, turning in measured slowness, gilding the undersides of clouds, probing at the edges of land and sky and sea.

But sailors far out to sea, I knew, could not see the long arms of the beacon. Just a flash as each beam turned to point straight at them. Fifteen seconds was our light station's signature. Every fifteen seconds, a *flash!*—visible for fifteen miles, showing seafarers where on the whole dark earth they were. Such a comfort, Papa said. Such an easing of the mind—to see the light, to count the seconds, to know without question, *This* is where we are. The beacon would show how to enter the harbor, if they were inclined. Most important: how to avoid the shoals.

After a time I climbed down to the service room, curled up in the heap of blankets Mama had given me. They were not *my* blankets, because Mrs. Wilton was sleeping in my bed. She had come to stay with Mama this night. When I'd asked if there was anything amiss, Papa had said no, just that a woman in Mama's *condition* should have help near at hand.

I nodded off a time or two, but cold seeped up through the iron floor and wakened me. Sometime during the night, after I had refilled the lamp and trimmed the wick, the wind picked up. Although a body could not hear it downstairs because of the thick stone walls, up here in the tower it whistled and moaned. The beacon flickered; I wrapped myself in a blanket and went to reset the vents. Steady again. Good. But now I would have to *watch*.

A faint glow had touched the sky above the redwoods to the east when I heard the first scream.

The sound jerked me to my feet, then held me frozen.

Footsteps below. Another scream: Mama. Then Mrs. Wilton was shouting: "Eliza! Come here!"

I threw off the blanket, pounded down the stairs. Lamplight in Mama's room. Mrs. Wilton, bending over her bed, twisted round to face me. "Is it safe to cross the isthmus?" she asked.

"I . . . I don't know."

"Go find out."

I stood stunned for a moment, unable to budge. "*Now*, Eliza. *Go!*"

There was something in her voice I had never heard before, something sharp and hard. It jolted me out of my trance. I fled downstairs, but it was too dark to make out the water level, too dark to read the clock. I fumbled with the matches, lighted a lamp. Eighteen minutes past four. When would the isthmus open up? Soon, I thought. But now? I didn't know.

Up again to the service room, find Papa's tide tables. Beside the long rows of figures indicating high and low tides Papa had printed the intervals when the isthmus would be clear: *4:33–7:15 A.M.*

Mrs. Wilton breathed out a harsh word when I told her—a prayer or a curse, I couldn't tell. Then, "Fetch me some towels. And scissors. Quickly!"

Down the stairs again. I snatched a handful of muslin towels from the linen closet, took the scissors from Mama's sewing basket, then climbed up two steps at a time. Through the doorway now, to the foot of Mama's bed.

Mrs. Wilton took the scissors and towels. "You must fetch the doctor the *instant* it's safe to cross. Do you understand?"

"But the beacon . . ." I couldn't leave the beacon. And with the wind picking up . . .

Papa had *entrusted* it to my care—and he was staying with the doctor. My heart shrank, thinking how he would look at me, on the mainland with the light untended.

"Oh!" Mama cried. She seemed to swallow a scream that escaped as a whimpering sob. Her face, at the dim edges of lamplight, looked white and clenched.

"Mama?"

Mrs. Wilton snipped at a towel, began to tear off a long strip. "Eliza, your mother is near death," she said grimly. "*I need help*. Go. *Now!*"

And there was a spreading stain on the bed near Mama's hips.

Blood. So much blood!

I turned, stumbled down the stairs, lighted the lantern by the door, threw on my slicker, and slid my feet into my boots. Outside, the wind sliced me to the bone. I fled down the slope to the isthmus. Fear poured through me and made me weak; my legs nearly buckled. The beacon raked through tufts of fog that scudded across rock and sand and water. Was the isthmus clear? Too dark to tell. But there. One of the tide rocks. Now above water. Now submerged.

Five minutes must have elapsed since I'd checked the clock. Maybe six; I'd forgotten to look again. Ten minutes early. A wet crossing. Papa strictly forbade me from crossing before the isthmus was dry, but he had done it, I knew.

Only in extremity. Only when he *must*.

I waited for a wave to draw back into the sea, then leaped, slipping and stumbling, from rock to rock. When the next wave came, it knocked me down into a tide pool. I gasped at the shock of cold, dragged myself out again, found another stepping stone, then another.

I turned back often to check the waves; their white crests loomed and vanished in the darkness like a flock of ghostly sheep. Each time I saw the beacon, I was glad. But now, with no one tending, it no longer seemed comforting. It seemed lonely. Frail. Once, I saw it flicker. I held my breath until it came back again strong.

Then I was slogging through water onto shore, soaked clear to my armpits. I cut between the driftwood heaps, struggling against my wet nightdress and slicker to scramble up the path to the top of the bluff, to run down the rutted dirt road to the doctor's house.

"Dr. Wilton!" I beat on the door. "Dr. Wilton, please come!"

I prayed for him to come quick, though dread squeezed down on my heart. I didn't want to face Papa. I pounded on the door again. "Dr. Wilton!" After an eternal wait I heard heavy footsteps and the scraping of the latch. The door creaked open; Dr. Wilton appeared in his nightshirt and shawl, his thin hair disheveled and sticking straight out on one side.

No Papa.

"It's my mother," I said. "She—"

"Is she bleeding?"

"Bleeding *bad!*"

"I'll dress and fetch my bag. Come in and wait—"

"I mustn't. I'm tending the light. Tell Papa to come too!"

I whirled round, half-glad that I wouldn't have to face him yet, then stopped.

The tower was dark.

Unthinkable.

I gaped at it. Then my feet began to stir, though my mind was still mired, still numb. Down the bluff, through heaps of driftwood, across the isthmus: this rock, that rock, jump across a stream. Now huffing up the path to the island, banging open the door. Put out the lantern, step out of my boots, hang my slicker on its peg, wring out my skirt.

"Eliza!" Mrs. Wilton called. "Is he coming?"

Mama. Oh, Mama.

"Yes," I called back. "Is Mama—"

She cut me off. "Fetch more towels!"

Back to the closet, snatch up an armful, then upstairs to Mama's room.

Mrs. Wilton, her hair coming loose from its knot, stood leaning over Mama, blocking my view of her.

"Is she—"

"Doctor'll see to her," Mrs. Wilton broke in. "Set the towels on the bed."

I turned to leave—*the beacon!*—then stopped cold. There was something in the washbasin on the table, something lying in a puddle of blood.

A baby. It must be a baby, though it looked

strange, like no baby I had ever seen. And tiny! I could have cradled it in two cupped hands.

"*Eliza, get out.* See to the beacon." Mrs. Wilton's voice was harsh, but I couldn't move, couldn't tear my eyes away.

It was curled up into itself, its too-big head huddled into its puny knees. Something white and creamy covered its skin, like an ointment; beneath, I saw a webbing of blue veins. Its mouth hung slack, as if it wanted to suck.

Mrs. Wilton draped a towel over the basin, took me by the shoulders, turned me toward the door. "Eliza, go!"

"Is it . . . dead?" I asked.

"She came too soon, wasn't ready for this world."

"Wasn't . . . ready?"

Mrs. Wilton pushed me firmly into the hall.

"But . . . Mama?" I twisted back; she was a lump under the quilt. My heart seized and stopped.

"Doctor'll see to her." Mrs. Wilton went back into the room, shut the door firmly behind her.

Numbly I climbed the stairs. All the hurry had been scoured out of me. I had to strike the match three times to get a light, then the draft blew it out, then I set the vents wrong and the flame blew out again. When I was setting on the chimney, it lurched out of my grasp and shattered. I had never broken a chimney! By the time I had retrieved a spare, the light was out again, and I had to begin anew.

When the beacon was lit—at last!—I took the spyglass and searched for boats. None on the rocks, praise God. But I could see a spray of moving lights on the dark water—fishing boats leaving harbor. They would know that the beacon had gone out, and they were bound to report it to the Lighthouse Service. At best, this would be a blot on Papa's record. He was so proud of his perfect record. At worst . . . I couldn't think of that now.

Where *was* Papa? Downstairs I could hear the doctor's rumbly voice—but not Papa's.

An image of the baby floated into my mind. *She*, Mrs. Wilton had said. My sister. *A spirited one*, Mama had called her. *A tad mettlesome*. Just this past week I had *felt* her, felt her move. And now she was dead.

Not ready for this world. Like a sea creature, who belonged in water and couldn't breathe out in air.

Footsteps on the stairs. Not Papa's. Mrs. Wilton looked up through the hole in the floor, from the service room. "Your mother's faring better, Eliza. We'll let her rest a spell, then take her across to the hospital. She's going to need some tending."

I nodded. Words wouldn't come.

"Here. You're shivering, dear. I fetched these from your room." She held up a bundle of dry garments.

I hadn't known I was shivering. I'd forgotten I was wet. But even after I'd put on the dry things—two pairs of woollen stockings, a flannel nightdress, my shawl—the shivering wouldn't stop.

Sometime after sunrise, when I was about to douse the beacon, I heard the front door open and the clump of Papa's footsteps on the stairs. Why had he been so long? He stopped in the bedroom for a spell, then climbed up again, to me.

I braced myself against his anger.

But he didn't look angry. His face sagged. He looked old.

"How long was it out?" he asked.

"Fifteen minutes, I calculate. Maybe twenty. No more'n that."

"There were boats." Not a question, but I could tell he wanted to know.

"None on the shoals! But in the harbor . . . lights were lit."

He nodded. I waited for him to reproach me, to scold me—anything but this silence. He just stood gazing out the window.

"Mama," I said. "She . . ."

He started up out of his thoughts, like he'd forgotten I was there. His eyes were sunken and hollow. He laid a hand on my shoulder, then stared out to sea again.

"You did right by her," he said.

7

R I L E D

Sometime during church the next Sunday I commenced to get riled.

It began when Pastor Applewaithe said our baby's death was for the best. But he didn't call her a baby. He asked folks to pray on account of "the tribulation of the McCully family." He entirely passed by the fact that our baby was a human soul, and she had died.

After the prayer Pastor Applewaithe said that God ordains everything, and everything he does is for the best, though we might not always understand his ways. Then we all stood and sang "A Mighty Fortress Is Our God."

I sat back down on the hard cedar bench next

to Papa. He took my hand in his: callused and strong, his neatly trimmed nails without a trace of dirt beneath them. Mama was still in the hospital. She was feeling poorly, Papa had told me.

The pastor commenced with the sermon. He was old, his voice thin and drowsy-making, like bees on a hot summer's day. Candles guttered and smoked; the odor of melting tallow mingled with the smells of wood polish and sweat. Mrs. Somersby shifted, creaking the bench in front of us; behind I heard a soft snore.

After a time we rose to read Mama's favorite psalm, the twenty-third. *The Lord is my shepherd. . . . I will fear no evil. . . . Surely goodness and mercy shall follow me all the days of my life.*

Light from the colored-glass window fell in splotches across the worn wooden floorboards in the aisle.

The red spots looked like blood.

When the service was over, Papa asked me to bide a spell while he spoke with Mr. Cuthbertson.

"Eliza?" Sadie, in her faded, Sunday-best frock, was pushing through the folks in the aisle, towing her five-year-old sister, Matty, behind. "I . . . I'm right sorry your ma's poorly," Sadie said.

I nodded.

"It . . . it happened to us, too, but then Ma had another'n."

All at once, to my shame, tears sprang into my eyes.

"Don't cry, Liza," Matty said. She said it *loud*. I swiped a hand across my cheeks—too late. Mrs. Overmeyer saw, and before I knew it, a flock of ladies had converged upon me, murmuring, shaking their heads, crowding out Sadie and Matty. "Such a trial." "So sorry." I nodded, said, "Thank you." But the anger was stirring, making a commotion inside me. And when Mrs. Somersby said that God sends trouble to make us strong, the blurts came on again.

"She wasn't a trouble," I said. "She was a *baby*." I turned to Mrs. Wilton. "You saw her. My baby sister *died*."

There was a sudden hush, a shifting, a flickering of glances.

Mrs. Wilton squeezed my arm. She looked at the other ladies and said firmly, "You're perfectly right, dear. She did."

Mrs. Wilton squired me round to the back of the line for the pastor. Sadie, I saw, had gone to stand with her family. Mrs. Wilton kept up a stream of comforting patter—about the weather,

her quilt making, parts of the sermon she'd cottoned to. But I could still hear tskings and scraps of talk from the ladies we'd left.

"Gone to a better place."

"Spared all this world's misery."

"The Lord couldn't bear to be apart from her."

"Something amiss, or he wouldn't have taken her away."

"A blessing—all for the best."

I knew they weren't trying to be cruel. But their words set up a churning, set up a racketing in my blood. The more I heard, the angrier I became.

And then I got mad at God.

Because none of it made sense. If he had wanted our baby with him, why did he lift up our hopes? Why did he make Mama scream, make her bleed? If he was perfect, as everyone said, why did he change his mind?

If he wanted to make us strong, why did he punish a helpless baby? It wasn't fair to sacrifice her life for us!

And how could it be for the best if there was something amiss with her? Why couldn't God just set her right? *That* would have been for the best!

I pressed down on these thoughts, tried to make them small. They were sinful, I knew.

When we reached Pastor Applewaithe, I twisted my mouth into a shaky smile. His eyes, the color of leather, searched my face. His bony hand squeezed mine. He said what a good, brave girl I was, with the *tribulation* and my mother laid up.

But later my anger began to leak out. I got mad at Parthenia when she escaped her pen the next day and spent the entire high tide wreaking havoc on the mainland. I got mad at Mama for staying at the hospital when I longed to have her home. I got mad at Mrs. Calhoun, who had come to keep house for us, she kept repeating, out of the goodness of her heart. She told me I was wasteful because I only picked at her stew. I told her the mutton was tough. She told me that sometimes our trials are punishments for our sins. Papa sent me to my room.

The next day Mrs. Calhoun was gone.

But up there in my room, I took the blue bottle from under my pillow and turned it over in my hands. What did the strange writing say? Was it some heathenish curse? Had I sinned by bringing it home?

When morning came, I took Papa's hammer from the shed, set the bottle on the rocks, and smashed it to smithereens.

❧ ❧ ❧

A week after the baby died, I fell to thinking about her body. Papa had told me we couldn't have a church funeral—it wasn't proper with babies born before their time. But I thought we could have our own service here, with just Mama and Papa and me, the way we had done when Pepper, a chipmunk who used to eat out of our hands, had died. We had put him in a tobacco tin and buried him on the island. I had set a smooth stone on his grave and laid flowers there from time to time. It seemed that was the least we could do for our baby.

But no one would tell me where she had gotten to. Papa wouldn't say. He told me to accept the will of God. Mrs. Calhoun—before she left—had scolded me for being morbid. I asked Mrs. Wilton about it when she brought us a meat pie for dinner one day. She said that the doctor had taken care of the body. That the family didn't bury in cases of miscarriage, she called it. It simply wasn't done. But she wouldn't tell me what *was* done.

Did the doctor just toss our baby onto the rubbish heap?

So then I got mad at *him*.

Now Papa seemed worried all the time: worried about Mama, worried about the inspector. He had written to the Lighthouse Service that the beacon had gone out, but he hadn't yet heard back.

"What will the inspector do?" I asked.

"He'll come to make inquiry, likelier than not."

"And what then? He wouldn't . . . make us leave?"

"Don't you trouble yourself about it," Papa said in a fierce, growly voice.

But I could tell that *he* was troubled.

You never knew when the inspector might come. Time was, whenever we spied him bound for the island, Mama would stoke up the cookstove and get cracking, whip up a pie. "*This* should sweeten him up," she would say. And it did, too. That—and Mama's Southern charm. Better still, for a good long while after the pie came out, the inside of the cookstove was too hot to inspect.

The house belonged to the Lighthouse Service, so the inspector pried into everything. Our inspector, Papa said, was more finicky than most. After checking the workings of the beacon, he stormed the living quarters. He checked the flour for weevils and the pump handle for rust. He checked the cookstove for proper blacking, the floors for sand and scratches, the ceiling for cobwebs, the windowsills for dust. He pored over every blessed inch of Papa's uniform, picking out the tiniest specks of lint, worrying over the straightness of every crease. He even inspected the privy!

Once, after the inspector had gone, I heard Mama say to Papa, "That man! I'm perfectly capable of keeping my own house!"

"This is more than an ordinary house, Rose," Papa had said. "Everything in a light station must always be shipshape!"

After Mrs. Calhoun left, it fell to me to keep it so. No time for school. Just stay at home and work. Two weeks after the baby died, Mama was still poorly and couldn't come home. I wanted to see her, but Papa, who visited her near every day, told me I must wait a little longer. "She's not herself yet, Eliza. You must be patient."

"Will Mama . . . die?" I asked. *That blood.* There had been so much blood!

"Whatever put that notion into your head?" Papa cried. "God wouldn't let that happen."

But he might. I knew it now. He *might*.

The church ladies were helping, fetching us meals, taking turns ironing Papa's shirts. Mary Connor still came on washday. But no one, save Mrs. Calhoun, could stay over from one low tide to the next, and she wouldn't anymore—or Papa wouldn't let her. I never found out which.

Work! So much work! It kept me hustling from sunup until well past dusk; I went to bed bone-tired.

Sometimes—when I was going to milk Parthenia or lugging a basket of wash to hang on the line—I would look out past the island to see dolphins leaping in the spray, or fishing boats scudding into port. Then I would feel such a longing to stay out in the fresh sea air, *witnessing* the world beyond our door.

There was no time, either, for helping Papa with the light. I was surprised to find that I scarcely minded. Some of the magic had leached out of the lighthouse and its workings. I had always felt so snug within those stout stone walls—even when the wind howled and green water boomed against the tower. Papa had assured me that we were safe in this house. These walls had withstood the fiercest storms the sea could heave at us, he said. Nothing could harm us here.

But if *this* could happen—this terrible thing—inside the very lighthouse walls . . . Well! Anything could happen. Nothing was safe, not in the whole of this wide world.

8

BITTER CUP

That night I woke to the sound of crying. I sat up in bed and strained to sort out the sound of it from the ones I knew well: the soft moan of wind up in the tower, the echoing clank of the clock-work, the creak and pop of metal contracting with the cold of night. The beacon passed my window, sent shadows swimming across the walls.

There was a baby in the house. I could hear it. I could make out the high, thin thread of its crying, weaving in amongst the wind sounds.

I pushed aside the cocoon of quilt and blankets, warm with body heat. I set my feet on the cold wooden floor. A chill crept between the threads of my nightdress, raised gooseflesh on my arms. Wild hopes went clattering through my sleep-fuddled mind—that the baby hadn't died, that she was somewhere in the house, that she was hungry. I would heat up milk and feed her. *Look*, I would say to Papa. *She's alive. Now all will be well again.*

I tiptoed across the landing, set my ear against Papa's door. Snoring. The crying didn't come from there. I could tell now. It was above, in the tower.

I felt my way up the steps. There was a greeny, echoey, underwater feel here, in the tower. I moved up toward the light.

Not in the service room. Nothing on the floor. Nothing on the bench, save what belonged there—the tin matchbox, the neat stack of folded polish cloths, the brass pitcher for filling the lamp.

Up the ladder to the top. Fog. Heavy fog all around. Pea-soup fog. It sponged up the beacon light, pressed it back, thick and bright, through the glass and into the room. I waded through waves of light, circled all the way around the lens.

Nothing here. No baby.

I stood listening again. The wind. Might it have been the wind?

But it had seemed so real. I had *heard* it!

Something inside of me cracked, caved in. I was a pure ninny, conjuring up fancies from my own longings! She was gone. Dead. I would never lay eyes on her again.

The letter from San Francisco came later than we expected—early in April, three weeks after the baby had died. The inspector was bound for the lighthouse, set to sail, most likely, on the *Elvina*. After that, I dusted twice a day, catching each speck of dust well nigh as it fell. I whisked away cobwebs while spiders were in the midst of spinning them. This would not count for much against the fifteen-minute gap, I knew. But I had to do something. Whatever I could.

And then, two days later, Papa said I could visit Mama.

Well. I *longed* to see her. Especially in the mornings, when I wakened thinking in the back of my mind that something good was coming, like Christmas. And then I would recollect myself: Baby's dead. Not coming ever. Mama's sick abed at the hospital. A sinking heaviness would settle over me, and I'd have to drag myself up through it to begin the day's work.

Mama looked pale. Dark circles ringed her eyes, and her blond curls hung limp about her face. But she smiled when I came in—a tad too cheery, I thought—and then embraced me so tight I could only just manage to breathe. Which was a comfort to me, beyond the mere embrace. Because if a body can clutch you that hard, she can't be *very* ill.

The bed slats creaked as I sat down beside her. There were two other beds in the room, but no one in them. All were spread with rough woollen blankets. Drab. It didn't seem a fit place for Mama, who favored pretty things—pinks and blues and lavenders, with lace aplenty. The only bright spot was the curtains, of yellow gingham, which Mrs. Wilton had sewn.

Mama squeezed my arm, rubbed it up and down. I breathed in the smell of rosewater— Mama's smell. She asked how I was getting on with Mrs. Calhoun and seemed surprised to learn she was no longer staying with us. "When did this come about?" she asked. "Who's minding the house?"

"We have help enough," I said. "The church ladies are cooking suppers and ironing Papa's shirts. Scarcely a thing for a body to do!"

Papa had told me not to worry her. *Take care what you say, Eliza Jane. Your mama's weakly now. She's frail.* It wasn't the time to complain about the work or ask about the baby's body.

But, "Scarcely a thing!" Mama said. "Mercy, child! Try to pull the wool over your very own mother's eyes! And Liza, what of school? Are you going to school?"

"Not just now, Mama."

Her eyes caught fire and she started to pull herself up in bed, so I went on real quick, "But I have my lessons for the next few weeks, and I'm doing them at night. I'm already far ahead."

"Don't you fiddle *me*, young lady. Out with the truth—all of it."

I couldn't help thinking that this was a change. Generally I told too much of the truth to suit her. But I only said, "Well, not *far* ahead. But I am caught up."

"Well." Mama sighed, sank back on the pillows. "Don't forget to go larking about the island from time to time, the way you do. All work and no play makes Jack a dull boy. Larking is good for the soul."

"Yes, Mama," I said. But I'd wait to go larking until the inspector had come and gone.

The door opened a crack and Dr. Wilton poked in his head. "Rose, have you drunk that tea? Oh, Eliza Jane, you're here! Good to see you."

"Thank you," I said.

The doctor glanced toward Mama's bed table. There was a bright, yellow-green liquid in a glass, not like any tea I'd ever seen.

"Have you tried it?" he asked.

Mama gave him her *look*.

"Now, Rose, this could help."

I recollected Mrs. Wilton at the China shanties, with the remedy for her constitution. Might this be . . . *Chinese* tea?

"I'll drink it, Guthrie. I promise."

"Good! Eliza Jane, will you stop by my office before you leave? There's something I want to show you."

"What is it?" I asked, suddenly afraid.

He flashed me his quick smile. "Come and you shall see!" He combed a finger through his mustache, cleared his throat. "Uh, and Eliza . . . how is your father?"

Mrs. Calhoun had told me that Papa and the doctor had had a set-to the night the baby died. It had been at the meeting about the Chinese. The doctor was soft on Chinamen, Mrs. Calhoun said.

Papa had been so het up he had refused to stay the night at the doctor's house and had gone home with Mr. Cuthbertson. That was why he'd been late coming home. No one would tell me what had been decided at the meeting about the Celestials—and now I scarcely cared.

Since then Papa and the doctor had spoken, but not often, I gathered. They tended to keep apart.

"He's well, thank you," I said.

"Give him my best."

After the doctor left, Mama shook her head. "Poor Liza. You need to tend to your Papa, too. He's not as strong as he seems."

I didn't understand. Papa not strong? He was the strongest person I knew!

Mama suddenly perked up. "Parthenia came here some days ago. I was sorely glad to see her—though I knew I shouldn't be. I heard laughter down the hall, then her mincing footsteps, and there she was! A little piece of home."

I felt a stab of jealousy. *Parthenia* had visited Mama, when I had not been allowed. And now, though I tried to swallow it down, an aching lump was rising in my throat.

"When are you coming *home?*" I asked, and I couldn't keep the aching out of my voice.

"It won't be long now," Mama said. "Doctor wants me to stay a spell, another week or so. I . . ." She broke off, gazed up toward the ceiling. Suddenly, she looked sad—her brave attempt at cheerfulness collapsing upon itself.

"Mama?"

She turned to me, shook her head. "Oh, Liza," she whispered. "It's such a bitter cup!"

I found Dr. Wilton bent over a microscope in his office. It was larger than his office at home, with a whitewashed floor, several wooden trestle tables, and banks of shelves along the walls. Some of the shelves were filled with books; others held ranks of brown glass bottles, clear jars full of metal instruments and cotton swabs, and stacks of small white enamelware trays and pans. The pleasant, woody aroma of pipe smoke all but crowded out the antiseptic smell.

He looked up when I pushed open the door. "Oh, Eliza, come see this."

But I couldn't. I couldn't force myself to be cheerful, as I had done for Mama, as she had done for me. I couldn't pretend that I cared about his silly contraptions anymore. My anger reared up and formed itself into a single question, blurted aloud: "Where is the baby?"

Dr. Wilton stared at me a moment, blinked.

"What did you do with the baby?"

He drew in a deep breath. "I buried her, Eliza, as I've done with all the others."

"The others?"

"The miscarriages. They're not unusual, Eliza. They happen. There are many women besides your mama who have miscarriage after miscarriage and . . ."

He stopped.

Miscarriage after miscarriage. "Did Mama have other babies too?"

Dr. Wilton hesitated. "That's for your parents to tell you. It's not my place."

"Then she did. Else you would have said *no.*"

He let out breath, seemed to sag a little. "Eliza, the others were at an earlier stage. You would not have seen . . . what you saw this time."

"I want to see where they are."

Dr. Wilton looked down, pushed a cork into a brown bottle on the table. He dumped the ashes from his pipe into a little saucer, then picked up a cloth and wiped his hands. At last he turned to me. "Very well," he said.

❦ ❦ ❦

Outside the sky had grown darker. Wind blew in fitful gusts, and clouds spattered bursts of pelting rain. We walked past the hospital to a patch of ground on the hillside, surrounded by a rickety picket fence. The sea grass grew sparser within the fence; the ground beneath had puckered into rows of little mounds, like kernels on an ear of corn. At one end of the nearest row there was a mound of fresh dirt.

I looked at it, turned to the doctor. He nodded.

So there you are, little one.

I wondered . . . what color would her hair have been, her eyes? Would she have had dimples when she smiled, like me?

"They're all . . . babies here?" I asked.

"All before their time."

To think that God had changed his mind all these many times. All that blood. All those tiny fingers and toes and ears. All those bitter cups.

"Where are Mama's other ones?"

He spread his hands, as if to encompass the whole of the enclosed plot. "They're . . . in amongst."

"You didn't mark them? You didn't keep an account?"

He shook his head.

A sudden wind gust whuffed past my ears and ruffled the sea grass, turning up its silvery undersides and flattening it against the hill. A flurry of raindrops pattered on my bonnet. Rain was splotching the doctor's coat, I saw. But he made no move to go.

I spun round and scrabbled about the hillside until I found a stone the size of my two fists put together. The anger inside me felt good. It felt strong. I opened the gate and set the stone at the foot of my baby sister's grave.

"There," I said to the doctor. "*Now* it's marked."

He nodded. "That's fine, Eliza." He turned, walked back toward the hospital. He looked shrunken somehow, bent against the wind. I recollected that he had been eager to show me something, and felt a little ashamed.

By the time I reached the bluff, the rain had evened into a heavy drizzle that blurred the horizon and turned everything gray. Tufts of fog blew in from the sea, scudded low across the isthmus. I picked my way among the heaps of driftwood and had nearly passed by the boulder where I had left the Chinaman's hat when I noted something odd: a pile of gravelly rocks atop it. I drew near, scraped away some of the rocks. Something underneath. Pushing aside the rest, I found a small oilskin pouch.

I untied the drawstring, tugged at the opening, poured the contents into my hand.

Seven pieces of Chinese ginger candy.

I had seen ginger candies at school when other children brought them. But I had never eaten one. *Shun all heathenish things.*

I turned my back against the wind and cupped the candies close to keep them dry. Such a beautiful gold color they were, encrusted with clear sugar crystals. They looked like treasure. Like a handful of gold nuggets. I brought them to my nose. The spicy smell of them made my mouth water.

Then something caught my eye, something else within the pouch. A rolled-up piece of paper.

I put the candy back in, drew out the paper. Stiff paper; it crackled when I unrolled it. Something drawn there. The drizzling rain made splotches in the ink, but I could still make it out. A girl's face, with braids and a bonnet—and tears running down her cheeks.

Me. It was me. I couldn't puzzle out just how I knew for certain—something about the shape of the face, the eyes, the mouth.

Me.

And grieving . . . Like I had a right to grieve. As if to say, what else would I do but grieve?

A tickling behind my nose; I blinked hard. Without thinking, I popped a candy into my mouth and began to chew.

It was sweet, tangy, good.

Still, Papa's words echoed in my mind. *Heathenish things.*

But lightning did not fall out of the sky and strike me down. The sea did not rise up to swallow me.

And then all at once I wondered: What if God wasn't keeping account of good and evil doings?

What if he just didn't care?

9

CHINESE MUST GO

The *Wing and Wind* sailed in from the south the next afternoon. As soon as the isthmus was clear, Papa sent me to town.

The inspector had written us he'd likely sail on the *Elvina*, but you never knew. "It might be best," Papa said, "if you were away when he comes to the island. Just this one time."

"Why?" I asked, a little hurt. Papa had always seemed so proud of me when the inspector came. "She's my best helper," he always said. Even though it made me abashed.

"Just this once. It's . . . ticklish this time. Pick up some muslin to replace the towels we lost. And see if Mrs. Cuthbertson's at the dry goods store.

You ought to get closer acquainted, because when the tides keep you on the mainland, you're to go to their house instead of the Wiltons'."

I was stung. "But why?" I asked again.

"It's settled," Papa said. "The Wiltons know my wishes and will send you there."

The Cuthbertsons! I was not fond of the Cuthbertsons. Mr. Cuthbertson was the proprietor of the dry goods store, and he eyed you sharp when you came in, like you were planning to steal him blind. He measured out the pintos so careful, you knew he'd begrudge you a single extra bean. Mrs. Winterberg once said she'd seen him setting his thumb on the scales, but Mama said that that was just gossip and not to repeat it. Mrs. Cuthbertson was a pinched woman who brought tiny portions of food to church suppers, saying that she and her husband were giving better than they got, because they ate scarcely a thing themselves.

"But the banner," I said, clutching at straws. "If I should become stranded on the mainland . . . you can't see the Cuthbertsons' house from here. How will you know I'm safe?"

"Tell Mrs. Wilton to hang the banner. But don't bide at their home."

83

I had gone to the Wiltons' house for years. I *liked* it at the Wiltons'. It didn't set right that because Papa had had a run-in with Dr. Wilton, I should be made to suffer.

Or was it, I thought, uneasy, because of *me?* Because of the blurts—my angry questions about the baby?

But no. There had been no time since yesterday for Dr. Wilton to talk to Papa.

Still, I recollected how the doctor had looked when I last saw him—shrunken and bent—and the shame of how I had treated him swept over me again.

It was one of those early-April days when rain squalls came scudding in from the west, their shadows skimming like sea skates across the surface of the water. Between the dark clouds were patches of clear blue sky. Now the sun was shining. Steam rose from rooftops, from puddles in the churned-up streets. A knot of fishermen and townsfolk had gathered on the dock, passing the time of day, watching the sailors unload a shipment of chickens and pigs. A rabble of gulls shrieked overhead. I looked hard but saw no one in the dark-blue Lighthouse Service uniform, with its rows of gold buttons. The afternoon stage rumbled past, splattering mud onto the plank sidewalk—and on the posse of boys and dogs who chased after it.

I purchased the muslin from Elsie Spooner, the clerk at the dry goods store. She wrapped it up with brown paper and string. I looked about for Mrs. Cuthbertson, but she was nowhere to be seen. Mr. Cuthbertson stood in his apron at the far end of the store. He was long-nosed and scarecrow-skinny, dwarfed by the man he was helping with hardware supplies. He nodded to me and smiled—puckerish, like he'd just swigged from a vinegar cruet—then went back to weighing nails.

"Eliza?"

I whipped round to see Sadie and Matty standing behind me.

"Parthenia's loose. I *think* it's her. Chowing down on Mrs. Calhoun's pansies."

I groaned.

"I'll help you catch her," Sadie volunteered. "If you like. Matty can fetch a rope from home."

It *was* Parthenia. By the time Sadie and I reached her, Mrs. Calhoun, wielding a broom, had driven off the goat, and she was tucking into the new-sprouted daylilies by the Pembertons' front stoop. I handed my parcel to Sadie, then ran at Parthenia, clapping my hands and scolding. That contrarious goat paid me no mind, but chomped off another lily. She chewed fast, side to side, waggling her long, scraggly beard. I grabbed her collar and tried to drag her away. "I'll tan your everloving hide," I muttered. Parthenia let out an indignant bleat and set her hooves. When I set *my* feet and pulled, she ducked her head, twisted away. The collar wrenched out of my hand; I went sprawling.

Sadie chased after, but she was no match for Parthenia. When *she* went down, she began to laugh, and then I was laughing too. There was nothing comical about the mangled flowers and the mud on our coats and frocks—and yet there we were, giggling like pure fools, chasing after that rattlebrained goat.

Matty soon caught up to us, waving a rope in the air. We surrounded Parthenia on three sides, I tied the rope around her neck, and the jig was up.

That's when I first heard the bell.

I looked at Sadie, puzzled. "I hear ringing."

"That's Horace Ahrens," she said. "Didn't you know?"

Horace? I shook my head. Horace was a farm boy, one of the older ones at school.

"Let's take a look-see!" Sadie picked up my parcel.

I hesitated. "I'd best fetch Parthenia home."

"Won't take more'n a minute." Sadie set off down the street toward the sound of the bell. "Wait for me!" Matty cried, and pelted after. Parthenia swiveled her ears, dropped a hill of pellets, then strained to follow.

I *was* curious. Why ever was Horace Ahrens ringing a bell?

Walking a goat through town is no straight-forward proposition. Bent on more shenanigans, Parthenia lunged forward, lagged back, lurched side to side. Anything that looked like food distracted her—flowers, tree bark, a dead fish. She reared up on hind legs, trying to get at Mrs. Hinkley's straw gardening hat, and near nibbled off the tip of Mrs. Plunkett's new silk scarf. In this part of town there were few sidewalks, mostly just muddy streets. I was glad when Sadie turned down H Street, toward the plank sidewalks farther down.

In front of the saloon I saw six or seven men, spitting and jawing. A little ways down, two doors from the China shanties on H and Second, a clump of schoolboys milled about. I picked out the gingery mop of Sadie's brother Samuel. He was two years younger than us and sat across the aisle from me at school.

And there, sure enough, was Horace, walking past the shanties, ringing a bell. "Chinese must go!" he called out. "Chinese must go."

My heart made a little stumble in my chest. Now I understood.

When I caught up to Sadie, I cinched the rope and took hold of Parthenia's collar. She shook her head, flapping her ears, but I held her fast. Matty tugged at my sleeve. "That's Mrs. Overmeyer's dinner bell," she said. "Samuel says Horace is getting a whole dollar every day."

A whole dollar! A fortune!

"Who's paying him?" I asked.

"Some of the townsfolk," Sadie said. "The Committee of Twenty-one."

"What's that?"

"They had a meeting. Some of the men. After Mr. Gartner hired the Chinese lumberjacks. They formed the committee then."

That meeting Papa had gone to. The one where he said they would decide what was to be done with the Celestials.

Sadie moved toward the schoolboys, bold as you please. I let Parthenia tow me along.

"Go home," Samuel shouted at Sadie. "And take Matty with you."

Sadie shifted my parcel to the front of her. "You can't boss me. I'm older'n you."

"This is no place for girls."

"This is no place for *little boys*," Sadie shot back.

There *was* an ominous look to things. The plank sidewalks in front of the China shanties stood empty. Doors shut, curtains and shades drawn. The shanties looked a mite sad to me now—with moss sprouting from their roofs and mildew growing on their peeling clapboards. They seemed to huddle together, like they were looking for comfort.

"Chinese must go!" Horace called again. "Chinese must go!"

"Are they in there?" I asked Sadie.

She nodded.

"How long has he been doing this?"

"Yesterday and today."

I glanced down the street a ways, at Sheriff Endert's house. No one home, looked like.

"What about the sheriff?" I asked.

Sadie shrugged. "Pa says he got to tread careful or blood could be shed. Tempers runnin' high."

The bell sounded over and over, like it was somebody's funeral. Like somebody had died. In one of the shanties I saw the corner of a curtain move aside. I thought about my China boy, likely trapped inside, likely wondering what would happen next. Was he scared?

I would be.

"Are they going to run them out? Like in Eureka?"

Sadie shrugged. She turned to look at me, suddenly grave. "Worse'n that been done. Up north, I hear tell, they burnt some Chinatowns clear to the ground. Over to Montana a whole gang of Chinese miners was killed."

"Why? What did they do?"

Sadie shrugged again. "Nothin'. Just worked for cheap, Pa says."

All at once Parthenia twisted behind me, away from the shanties. I wheeled round, hauling back on her rope, to see a Chinaman carrying a plump little pig and limping down the street toward us. He was old and gaunt, with a long gray mustache and a thin pigtail hanging down his back. I recognized him then. The man from the herbalist's shop. The China boy's grandfather.

"Hey, John Chinaman." Amos Tyler brushed past us, sauntered to the middle of the street. Jug-eared Stephen Somersby followed behind. They stood blocking the Chinaman's way.

Parthenia strained toward the Chinaman. She jerked her head up and down, trying to get loose. That straw hat, I thought. She hankered to chomp on that hat.

The bell clanging faltered as Horace got wind of the turn things were taking. For a moment he seemed not to know what to do. Then he turned his back on the trouble and began ringing down the street. Horace was not purely mean, like Amos and Stephen. But that dollar likely pulled at him hard.

I looked at the men by the saloon. Appeared they saw what was coming, but they weren't making any moves.

Now the Chinaman had neared Amos and Stephen. He said something soft-like to the boys—I couldn't hear what. Then he walked to the far side of the street, tried to go by.

Amos moved to block him. The Chinaman stopped, walked back toward us. Now Stephen moved to block him.

The Chinaman feinted left, then tried to run

between the boys. Amos dashed toward the old man, rammed him headlong into the muddy street. The pig broke loose and ran. Stephen dived for it, caught it by a rear leg. The pig set up an earsplitting squeal.

Parthenia changed her tack; she backed into me, ears flattened against her head. I saw Matty slip her hand into Sadie's. Samuel looked like he might want to do the same, but his pride wouldn't let him.

"You want your pig, John?" Amos asked. He stepped between the Chinaman and the pig. The Chinaman got to his feet.

The pig's squealing must have drowned out the sound of doors and footsteps, because now, across the street, I saw a scuffle on the boardwalk in front of the China shanties. Two Chinamen were holding a third by the arms. The third one tried to break loose, but the others were bigger. . . .

He was a boy, the one they were holding. He looked up quick and something jolted through me. *My China boy.* I shrank back, hoping he hadn't seen me.

Three more Chinamen came out onto the sidewalk. I recognized the second old man from the herbalist's shop. The round one, who had been smiling. He wasn't smiling now. He limped up to the China boy, set a hand on his shoulder, said something in his ear. The boy shrugged off the hand but stopped struggling. The Celestials were looking at one another, looking at the old man in the street, looking at the men by the saloon. Dread lay like a stone in my belly. Knowing about Eureka. Knowing about the burnings, the killings.

What would happen if they tried to rescue the old man? Some of the men by the saloon were armed. . . .

"Chinese must go!" It wasn't Horace; it was one of the schoolboys near me. I was afraid the others might join in, but they didn't.

"C'mon boys, leave him be." Mr. Sawyer had stepped away from the men by the saloon. "Amos? You hear?" One of the men said something to Mr. Sawyer; he frowned and turned back toward the saloon.

"Come get your pig, John," Amos called.

The Chinaman looked at his pig, then back at Amos. He didn't move.

"What's the matter—you scared?" Amos picked up a rock and winged it in the direction of the pig. The rock hit down a scant foot away, splattering the pig and Stephen with mud and starting up a louder spate of squealing.

"Hey!" Stephen said. "You're like to hit *me*." He was having trouble holding on. He had managed to get a grip on the pig's middle and had lifted it onto his lap. But the pig was bucking its whole body, flailing its sharp little hooves. Stephen looked as if he were tiring of this game.

Amos picked up another rock. "I don't think your pig likes rocks, John. You better come rescue it."

I glanced toward the China boy again. *He was looking at me.* His eyes flicked away; a wave of heat flooded my face. I hadn't a blessed thing to do with this, and yet it must have seemed that I held with Amos and Stephen—just by being here, just by doing nothing.

Parthenia lunged; I unclasped my fingers, let the rope slip burning through. With a bleat of pure joy she made a beeline for the Chinaman's hat. Amos, whirling to look, stumbled; the old Chinaman hobbled past him, with Parthenia hot on his heels. I never saw a body hobble so fast. Amos went for him, but too late; he got an armful of goat. Parthenia turned, put her head down, butted Amos flat on his back. Then the pig was somehow loose, and Stephen fleeing. Two Chinamen ran to the old man, took hold of his arms, then hoisted him up to the boardwalk and through a doorway. The China boy caught the pig, wrestled it through the same doorway. The door closed. Parthenia stood outside on the walk, bleating piteously. From inside the shanty I could hear the pig's muffled squeals.

Mr. Sawyer had come up. "That's enough," he said. "It's over. Horace, get to work, son. The rest of you skedaddle on home."

I ran to fetch Parthenia. Sadie came to help, and Matty followed. We dragged Parthenia off the boardwalk and into the street. The other boys had scattered, but not Amos. He stood waiting. As we passed he narrowed his eyes at me.

"You!" he said. "You better keep hold of that gol dern goat."

Parthenia was even more cantankerous than usual going home. And the heavy parcel I was carrying didn't help. Another squall had blown in, hurling wind and rain into my face, and Parthenia kept yanking me off balance into one plaguey tide pool after another.

By the time we reached the island, the bottom

half of my skirt was sopping and crusted with sand—not to mention my coat, where I had sat plunk down in the muddy street.

"You're a blamed nuisance," I told her when at last we reached her pen. But I gave her bony backside a little pat. She butted me gently; I stroked the bristly hair between her ears and then, gathering my skirts, leaned down and scratched her favorite place, between her cloven toes. She closed her eyes; her sides heaved in a contented sigh. "Well," I said. "Still. I reckon you showed that Amos a thing or two."

I had just taken off my boots and coat inside the house when I heard voices. Not the inspector, surely! It couldn't be. I hadn't *seen* him on the dock. . . .

Now the voices grew louder; footsteps rang on the stairs.

Might I have missed him? Had he been in the ship still when I'd passed?

I ran to the closet to put away the muslin, then felt something gritty underfoot. Sand! I had forgotten to brush it off my skirt; it had scattered all across my new-waxed floor. I fled to the kitchen, brushed off my skirt as best I could, then wet a dishrag and set to work on the sitting room floor.

I was kneeling, swabbing hopelessly at the sand, when Papa and a tall, stern, blond-bearded man in a Lighthouse Service uniform emerged from the stairway. The inspector. Inwardly I groaned. I stood, smiled, thrust the dirty cloth behind my back.

"Oh, Eliza, you're here," Papa said. "Inspector, you remember Eliza Jane."

"Of course." He turned to me. His eyes were the palest blue; I could never read them. "I'm sorry to hear of your family's troubles, Eliza Jane."

I swallowed, dipped my head. "Thank you kindly."

Then they were moving toward the front door. I winced at the crunch of sand beneath their boots.

Papa walked the inspector down to the isthmus; they stayed there and talked for a spell. I mopped up the sand, tried to collect my wits. *Supper. Start fixing supper. Peel the potatoes.*

When Papa returned, he seemed sober but not grim.

"I didn't know he was here," I said, "or I'd have stayed away. I didn't see him—"

"It was fine," Papa said.

"What did he say? About the beacon going out?"

"He was . . . mindful of the circumstance," Papa said. "Sympathetic. But he doesn't want to see it happen again. He . . ." Papa paused. "He feels you're too young to tend the light alone."

The old, familiar anger beat against me in waves. I hacked at the potato, taking off big, wasteful chunks along with the peel. *It wasn't my fault*, I thought. *I couldn't be two places at once. No one could. Besides, if you hadn't been so set against the Celestials, you would have been home.*

"We can stay," Papa continued, "though there's a blot on my record. And the inspector made it clear: we have no room for further missteps."

1 0

Get You from Me

Papa came back from town the next afternoon steaming mad. "Henry Tyler told me you were interfering with the doings at the China shanties," he said. "I told him you wouldn't do such a thing, that you'd never tarry thereabouts, much less interfere. But he rounded up Amos and Stephen Somersby, and they upheld the tale. I don't know what to think. Eliza, what have you to say?"

"I was there," I admitted.

"And you *interfered?*"

I could see that Papa wanted to believe there had been some misunderstanding, or even that Amos and Stephen had lied. I recollected how my fingers had unclasped from Parthenia's rope.

I could say it was an accident, that she had pulled too hard. But I knew that *I* had unclasped my fingers, that I had wanted to stop Amos and Stephen.

"Yes," I said.

Papa gaped at me. He shook his head as if to clear it. "What in heaven's name possessed you?"

So I told him the whole story. He heard me out to the bitter end, looking grimmer by the moment. His brows furrowed together, making a thick, dark ridge above his eyes.

"Now you've made a complete and utter fool of me!" I recoiled from the heat in his voice. "I hold a respected position in this town. I've taken a public stand against the Celestials, and now my very *daughter* is undermining me. It's a mortification. You've sullied my good name."

The unfairness of this stung. "But Amos and Stephen are bullies!" I said. "They were badgering an old man who had no defenses. You always told me, Papa, to find courage to stand up to bullies."

"This is different. What Amos and Stephen did was merciful in the long run because it will encourage the Celestials to leave before the townsfolk are forced to take measures."

"Take measures?"

"Run them out. As the good folk did in Eureka."

"Then I think *that* would be bullying," I said. "They haven't shot anyone here. They haven't harmed a soul."

"Haven't harmed a soul? Henry Tyler's out of a job, girl! He's got seven mouths to feed. If that's not harmed, I don't know what is. And a heap more men—good Christian men—will be out of work soon if we don't put an end to this. Those heathens would snap up every job in town if they could—and send California gold across the sea to China. Or smoke it up in those opium dens they've got. They're a fester upon the township!"

I felt battered by the anger in his words. I wished I could agree with him, take it all back, ask for his forgiveness, make his anger go away. It was right that I should do so.

And there was truth to what he said. Henry Tyler losing his job—that was a bad thing. And Sadie . . . I worried about her papa too.

But Papa had put by a truth *I* had to tell—a truth that ran counter to his. He had come down on the side of bullies.

"They're heathens, Eliza Jane. They contaminate

us all, just being near. By tolerating them, we are shunning God."

And then something slipped between my lips before I could stop it. "Look what God did to our baby. Maybe he deserves to be shunned."

Papa's silence frightened me. He backed up a pace and stared. Then, "Get you from me," he said. "I can't be near you now. Get out of my sight!"

I left.

Papa did not intend, I knew, to force me out of doors. My banishment was from his presence only; he meant for me to go to my room. But there was so much anger in me, it seemed to swell up my whole body and smoke out through my skin. I couldn't stay in the house; it would fill up with my poisons.

The tide had begun its uprise, but I didn't care. If it shut me out tonight, well, let Papa cook his *own* supper!

I crossed the isthmus and struck north along the beach. At first I just *walked*—as fast as I could. The wind buffeted me from behind, set my coat and skirts to flapping. It raised whitecaps in the flinty sea and tossed streaming combs off the breakers. Bits and pieces of our quarrel went racketing about my mind. *A mortification. Merciful in the long run.*

How could cruelty be a mercy? For it was cruel, what Amos and Stephen had done. Even though Amos's father had lost his job—a terrible thing—that old man had had nothing to do with it. And crueler still were the *measures* Papa spoke of: uprooting the Celestials and drumming them out of their very homes. Even Pastor Applewaithe spoke of converting heathens, not running them out.

But it was my own words that swept back on me most often: *Maybe he deserves to be shunned.* Oh, I was wicked to say such a thing! Why couldn't I hold my tongue?

But I had *thought* it before this—or something very like. And saying it, laying tongue to the blasphemous notion, had sent a strange thrill through my body. A feeling of power. A feeling of truth.

Would God punish me for this?

I had always felt comforted by God, cradled in the warmth of his love. *The Lord is my shepherd; I shall not want.* He would punish evildoers but protect and reward the good. And I had been so certain which was which.

But now . . . it wasn't clear at all.

And which was I?

The virtuous will have their reward in heaven, Papa often said. But to my mind, that couldn't varnish over what happened here.

And heaven . . . who had truly *seen* heaven?

Then another notion occurred to me. What if God were nothing more than a hopeful story we told ourselves? Just a *wish*—that if we prayed, if we followed the Commandments and repented when we slipped, no harm would befall us. That if we were good, we would be loved and sheltered and cared for—not cast adrift on a cold, wide sea.

I was surprised when I found myself past the next cape, well beyond sight of the lighthouse. I had paid scant heed to my surroundings—nor to time or tide. Though earlier I had thought about staying off the island all night, now . . . I wanted to go home. The sun had slid far down the sky; I could see by a brightness behind the clouds that it would set before long.

The tide had risen alarmingly.

I turned for home, but now the wind was against me. It numbed my face and whipped clean through my good woollen coat. It kicked up sand, flung it in my face. It pressed me back; I had to lean into it and push to move ahead at all. Slow. I was forever rounding the cape. When at last I reached the isthmus, the path was underwater, with waves breaking across from both sides.

Worse than a wet crossing. Even Papa wouldn't attempt this.

If only I might go to the hospital, see Mama! I could tell her my troubles. I could sleep on the floor beside her.

But . . . Papa was trying so hard to protect her from worry. Poorly as she was, it wouldn't be right to burden her with this.

I stood leaning against the wind, gazing homeward across the drowned isthmus. Rocks clanked and grumbled—a mournful, hollow sound. Our house looked tiny on its hump of an island. As I watched, the beacon flickered to life, then stretched its long arms across the water. I could see Papa in the tower, silhouetted against the light. I wondered if he saw me.

He would be *very* angry now.

Mrs. Wilton met me at the door before I'd even knocked. She smothered me in a soft, lavender-smelling hug, then shooed me inside. "Praise heaven you're here, Eliza," she said. "Your papa is beside himself." She motioned me to the sitting room, brought me a cup of milk and a plateful of apple dowdy, then bustled back out to hang the banner from the porch.

"What . . . what did Papa say?" I asked when she returned. Here, beside the crackling fire, with apple dowdy warm inside me, what I had said about God seemed scandalous. What would Mrs. Wilton think of me if she knew?

"Child, he's worried sick! By the time he discovered you were gone, the tide was flooding the isthmus. He came here searching, but had to go back. The doctor has gone looking for you in town, though your papa wouldn't ask him to."

"They're still . . . feuding?"

Mrs. Wilton sighed. "It's somewhat eased. I'm thinking they'd both like to bury the hatchet, but you know how men are. So fond of being *right*."

I pictured Papa worrying about me and felt glad in a mean, small way—but guilty at the same time. More than that, relieved. He didn't want me *from him* anymore.

"Did he tell you about . . . the China shanties?" I asked. "About what I did?"

She raised her eyebrows. "He didn't have to, Eliza. The whole town knows."

"Well, what do you think? Was I wrong to . . . to interfere? That pitiful old man . . ."

"Oh, my dear." Mrs. Wilton patted my hand. "I'll not be inserting *my* notions between you and your father. You can patch things up, the two of you. He loves you something fierce."

Dr. Wilton soon returned. I was a little worried about seeing him again, after the last time. Seemed like I was provoking folks right and left—blurting up a storm—these days. But he soon put me at ease. He told me Mama was improving, that she would be coming home soon.

"How soon? Tomorrow?"

"Can't make any promises. And you'll still have to do for her, Eliza, when she's home. She's weakly yet."

I was hoping I could stay with the Wiltons that night. But the rift between Dr. Wilton and Papa had not been mended so far. They must honor Papa's wishes and take me to the Cuthbertsons'. I couldn't even stay to supper, though Mrs. Wilton, adhering to the letter but not the spirit of the law, kept plying me with food that didn't count, she said, as supper: corn muffins, hot cocoa, stale bread-and-cake pudding. By the time she wrapped me in my coat, lent me her rain bonnet, and set me out the door with Dr. Wilton, I couldn't have stuffed more victuals down my gullet if I'd tried.

I turned back once to look at the beacon. Raindrops shimmered in its long, pale beam, then vanished when it passed. The tower looked sad, somehow. Forlorn.

I wondered if Papa was lonely.

Dr. Wilton had a comfortable, rolling gait that was easy to keep pace with. He was easy to talk to, too. Before we had crossed B Street, I found myself apologizing for my ill manners the other day. He waved my words aside. "It's a hard thing, what happened. I'd be angry too."

A lump rose in my throat; I swallowed. Angry at whom? I wanted to ask. At God?

It would be a comfort to know that someone else felt that way. That I wasn't the only one. It would be . . . less frightening somehow. But I couldn't work up the gumption to ask him straight.

We stepped up from the muddy street to the sidewalk. In the shelter of the buildings the wind, which had calmed somewhat from before, abated further still.

"I *would* like to see what you were going to show me," I said. "In your microscope."

"I'll have to speak with your father about that. I'm certain he'll come round, in time. Patience, Eliza."

It was quiet now. The streets were dark and nearly empty. The windows in the undertaker's parlor and newspaper office had gone black, but lamplight seeped between the curtains of the houses. Our boots clunked on the planks. Beyond there was only the distant, tinny music from a saloon, the patter of rain on the roofs, the rumble of the sea, and the wind. The air smelled fresh, of fir.

Suddenly I turned to Dr. Wilton. "Why are you and Papa feuding? Is it because of the Celestials?"

"Eliza Jane, it would be interfering for me to discuss this matter with you."

"Well, I've been thinking. It doesn't seem right to punish the Celestials because of what happened to Amos's father. It's not their fault. They need jobs to live too. And that poor old man . . ."

The doctor grunted but said nothing.

"Maybe they're wicked because they don't believe in God. But—"

"They don't believe in *our* God. Or at least, not precisely as we do. Some have a concept of heaven, that it guides their lives. Some believe in many gods."

"Oh!" This was something new. *Many* gods. Or guided by an alien, godless heaven. So lonesome that would be! But still . . .

I plunged ahead. "What if they don't know any better? What if they're just honoring what their parents told them? You're bound to do that—the Bible says. And is it our place to punish, to be cruel? Jesus said, 'Blessed are the merciful,' and . . ."

Dr. Wilton was shaking his head—in a resigned way, not as if he were saying no. "Different folks look to different parts of the Bible to guide their lives."

"I don't understand."

"Some folks dwell on the parts that condemn heathens. And those parts are there, of a surety. Other folks look to the parts that say all men are brothers, and that you're bound to help even people whom you consider to be sinners."

I pondered that for a moment. "Then how is a body to know which parts to go by?"

Dr. Wilton laughed. "Ah, Eliza! Wiser men than I have spent the whole of their lives on that question!"

I I

ILL NIGHT

The Cuthbertsons seemed surprised to see me. "Eliza!" Mrs. Cuthbertson said with a start. You'd think she'd seen a ghost. Mr. Cuthbertson led the doctor to the far side of the porch and spoke to him low. I thought I heard him say, "It's an ill night for this." Dr. Wilton cut me a sidelong glance and said something I couldn't make out; Mrs. Cuthbertson shooed me into the house, saying they'd had supper but that if I liked, she could boil me up some cornmeal mush.

I told her I wasn't hungry.

Mrs. Cuthbertson made no move to settle me abed. She set her spectacles on the end of her nose, threaded a needle and set to darning.

Presently the doctor and Mr. Cuthbertson came in. Dr. Wilton cleared his throat. "Eliza," he said, "there's been a change. Come along." He nodded at the Cuthbertsons and guided me out.

"What's amiss?" I asked as the door shut behind us.

Dr. Wilton let out a deep, groaning sigh. He turned to me and smiled, sort of rueful. "It's only for tonight. I pledged I wouldn't say."

My gaze slid past him. The saloon bled light into the rain-dimpled puddles on the street; I could hear music and voices inside. A little way down, the China shanties stood black and silent. Horace Ahrens had gone home.

"Might I stay at your house, then?"

He took out his pipe, filled it, tamped it down. He looked tired. "*I'd* prefer it. But I don't want to violate your father's trust—all the more now, when there's hope of mending fences. Is there anyone else you could stay with, someone your folks would approve of?"

I felt like Mary and Joseph with no room at the inn. "Well, there's the Pembertons. Mrs. Pemberton and Mama are good friends. And they're just a couple of doors down."

"Hmm." Dr. Wilton lit his pipe and puffed on

it, filling the night air with fragrant smoke. He stepped out to look at the Pembertons' house.

"Or the Gumps," I said hopefully. Mama didn't wholly approve of Sadie. *Like* her—that she did. A body couldn't help it. And she was glad that we were friends. But Sadie's grammar and manners . . . well. She was not as much of a *lady* as Mama would have preferred.

"They're over to Fifth Street, aren't they?" the doctor asked.

"Yes. Far side of the courthouse."

"Let's mosey in that direction," he said. "If that doesn't pan out, I'm taking you home with me."

Mrs. Gump opened the door. She was burping a baby over her shoulder. Two ginger-haired children peered out from behind her skirts; another one came crawling through the threshold, but she blocked it with a well-placed boot. Dr. Wilton explained the situation, and Mrs. Gump smiled. Two of her teeth were missing. "Sadie'll be pleased as punch," she said. "Sadie! Sadie, see who's come!"

It was a good thing the Gumps didn't keep a light station. With nine children underfoot and Mr. Gump up to the lumber camp, Mrs. Gump appeared to have thrown up her hands and given tidiness the go-by. The children did seem loved—but wild. Although Sadie lent a hand—washing dishes, changing diapers, spooning gruel into little mouths—there was always more *un*done than done. I had thought the Gumps clannish, but at home they were far from cordial to one another. And such a racket! Squealings, tauntings, tattlings, tiffs! They put me in mind of seagulls squalling round a fishing boat come into port.

I helped Sadie and her mother tuck in the younger ones for the night. Then, wearing a borrowed nightdress, I bedded myself down between Sadie and Matty on a lumpy straw tick that was none too clean.

I couldn't get to sleep. Chill air seeped in through the thin, scratchy blanket. Little groaning, snuffling sounds came from the other side of the room, where two of Sadie's sisters slept on a narrow cot and one lay on a blanket on the floor. Matty *squirmed;* she poked me once with her sharp little elbow and kicked me twice. Something tickled in my nose. Dust. Well, dusting was likely last on Mrs. Gump's list.

From the kitchen I could hear the clank of a

stove lid, the squeak of the pump. Presently Mrs. Gump's footsteps went past, and a door thumped shut. In a moment I heard snoring, then it tapered off.

No sooner had the house fallen silent than my mind commenced to stir itself up. I stewed about Papa in the lighthouse, worried and alone. About Mama in the hospital, still poorly. Just as I got round to fretting about why I couldn't stay at the Cuthbertsons' on this *particular* night, there came a creak, then the pad of bare feet in the hall outside our door.

Sadie sat bolt upright. In the moonlight that leaked through the crack between the curtains, I could see her set a finger to her lips. She threw aside the blanket and tiptoed to the door. Then she motioned me to come.

"What is it?" I whispered when I was near.

"Shh!" She opened the door, tiptoed down the hall. Beyond her I heard the front door thud shut.

I found her sitting on a stool near the heap of shoes and boots beside the door. She pulled on a shoe and began to button it. "Better put yours on," she hissed. "And your coat."

I crouched beside her. "Why?" I whispered back. "You're not going out, are you?"

"Samuel did. He's been freakish all day. He's got the look-arounds, and I aim to find out why."

"But I don't think you should—"

"He thinks he's so big. Always sayin', with Pa gone, he's the man of the house. Always tellin' me what *girls* can't do. Well, I'm older'n him. I can do anything he can, and then some. 'Sides, I figure, bein' older, it's my job to keep an eye on *him*. Get your boots on, Liza! Time's wastin'!"

A cough from a back bedroom. We froze. There was a rustling sound, then silence, then snoring again.

"Are you . . . *allowed* to go out at night, to find Samuel?" I breathed.

"Course not! We'll get a lickin' if Ma finds out." Sadie seemed mighty cheerful about the prospect.

She stood and shrugged into her coat. "Ain't you comin'?"

I could see by the look in her eye that I might as well save my breath. Nothing I could say would change her mind. And I purely couldn't stomach going back to that bedroom alone. What would I tell Mrs. Gump if she awoke and found Sadie gone? That I knew she'd left the house and didn't tell? But I didn't want to tattle on her either . . . nor on Samuel.

I reached for my boots.

The rain had ceased; raggedy clouds swam across the face of a moon coming on to full. Beyond the fresh scent of fir something burnt prickled my nose. The street stood dark and empty; we could not see where Samuel had gotten to. But a faint halo of light rimmed the buildings to the south. And the rumbling of many voices told us where to look.

Second Street. The China shanties.

A shiver passed through me, raised gooseflesh on my arms.

I reckon I had known, from the moment the Cuthbertsons turned me away, what was to come this night. I hadn't wanted to think on it. I had wanted it to pass, with nothing to do with me.

But now I trotted along beside Sadie, pulled toward the voices like flotsam on an incoming tide.

When we turned the corner to H Street, I could see the torches farther on—a score of them at least—a river of light and shadow surging toward the China shanties. Sadie began to run, and then I was running too—we and the torches and the men all flowing together, converging upon the same dark calamity.

Around the corner now, to Second Street. The sounds welled up: shouting, a drumbeat of footsteps, torches crackling, horses whinnying. No music came from the saloon, and the downstairs lights had been doused. Now I could make out two wagons, and horses, and, in the torchlight, some of the men's faces: Mr. Hinkley struggling with the reins of his team, Mr. Cuthbertson letting down the tailgate.

I looked across to the sheriff's house and saw him, or someone, standing on his front stoop. Two men—holding clubs?—blocked his path. *Tempers running high. Blood could be shed.*

Sadie stopped just around the corner, in front of the Cuthbertsons' house. "Do you see Samuel?"

I shook my head. I wasn't looking for Samuel anymore. I smelled horses and smoke and stale whiskey; my eyes searched the dark for the China boy.

Someone screamed. Down the street, two men were dragging a Chinese woman toward us. "Please," she cried. She was clutching something, a heap of blankets. "Please." The men hoisted her roughly into the wagon. Behind came another man with two small children, one tucked under each arm. He heaved them into the wagon; they ran to the woman, huddled in her arms.

More Chinese were coming—four or five women pushed and dragged to the wagons, a dozen children lifted, shoved inside. Their pleas and cries wrung my heart. The horses snorted and stamped; the drivers cursed as they tried to control them. Back at the shanties I could hear shouting. Chinese men, held back by white men with guns.

And there was Amos Tyler, prodding two old men with a stick, as if they were sheep or cows. A stooped, gaunt old man. A short, round old man with a bad limp. From the herbalist's shop. From the bell ringing. Both tottered under the weight of huge, lumpy bundles. I stepped forward, wanting to do something, but then stopped, afraid. Amos must have seen movement, because he turned to face me. He looked startled, then glared.

One of the horses whinnied and lunged; the wagon lurched; the people inside stumbled and screamed. The stooped old man's bundle had burst; its contents went clattering down the open tailgate as Amos and Mr. Cuthbertson shoved him up into the wagon. Pots, bowls, ladles, knives, blankets, an odd-looking stringed instrument. The round Chinaman was talking to Mr. Cuthbertson—pleading, I could tell, to be able to pick up the thin man's possessions. All he had left in the world, most like. But Mr. Cuthbertson only shouted at him. Then more white men were coming. They pushed the round Chinaman and his bundle into the cart, trampling the other man's belongings. A heavy boot stomped down on the instrument, snapping its neck.

"Eliza!" Sadie was tugging at my elbow. "Eliza, come along!" She pulled me around the corner; we squatted under the overhang of the Cuthbertsons' front porch. "Did you see how he looked at you?"

"Who?" I asked.

"Amos. He's *riled.*"

I heard the drivers shout and the crack of their whips. The wagons lurched forward, and the Celestials disappeared beyond the Cuthbertsons' porch. But I could hear them still—their voices rose together in a great, aching wail.

12

MISERY AT A DISTANCE

We left soon after the wagons did. The mob looked to be breaking up; best to hasten back before it scattered all through the streets.

Sadie and I crept into the house without rousing her mother. Matty groaned when we slipped in beside her. She flung out a hand, clouting me in the eye, and began snoring softly. Presently I heard Samuel come in; soon after, Sadie's breathing grew slow and regular.

But I couldn't sleep for the worries that leaped about my mind.

Fire. Those Chinatowns up north, Sadie said, burned to the ground.

Killings. The miners in Montana . . .

The women and children. Where had they taken them? What would they do with them?

The China boy. A remembering swam into my mind—of him sopping wet, holding Parthenia in his arms. Where was he now? What would become of him?

I told myself that there was nothing I could have done. Come what might, I couldn't have stopped them. But I felt . . . wrong someway. Sullied. To have watched such a thing in silence.

I did fall asleep at last, for I recall Sadie shaking me to rouse me. I managed to sit up, but my belly set to churning, and my limbs went weak, and something heavy rolled round inside my skull. Sadie called for her ma, who took one look and made me lie back down again. I don't recollect Sadie leaving, nor Matty, either. I don't recollect *much* until the doctor came. He listened to my chest and dosed me with something bitter, then said he was taking me to the hospital.

"She's that bad?" I recollect Mrs. Gump asking.

"Not bad at all. But she can rest there with her mama until low tide. I'm thinking there'll be two exiles returning to the lighthouse today."

It took me a moment—my head was that addled.

Then, "Mama . . ." I said. "Is she . . ."

The doctor nodded, gave my shoulder a squeeze. "Yes she is, Eliza Jane. Your mama's going home."

At the hospital Mama made a fuss. This time *I* lay in bed while she sat on the blanket, stroking my hair. I breathed in deep, savoring the lovely rosewater smell of her. "You're going to be fine," she kept saying. "Everything's going to be fine."

I didn't want to dispute with her. *She* seemed well—in good spirits, her color back, so changed from before. Despite my queasy stomach and the pounding in my head, I felt hope flooding the empty spaces in my heart. Mama home. Mama back to herself again.

But . . . *fine?* Didn't she know what had happened last night?

And had she forgotten our baby—so soon?

Later, when I was coming up out of sleep, I heard Papa's voice. Dread clutched at me. Was he still angry? And . . . Amos. Had he told anyone I'd been near the China shanties this past night? Did Papa know?

I kept my eyes shut, listening. Papa was a little way off, talking to Mama. Their voices were soft; I couldn't make out what they were saying. But he didn't sound angry—not at all.

I let out a slow breath, then opened my eyes.

He came to me at once. He kissed the top of my head, then pulled up one of the hospital's wooden chairs and sat down. "How are you feeling?" he asked. His voice was gentle. He smelled of turpentine and soap.

"Better," I said. Not much, but I knew he didn't like complainers.

"Eliza." Papa took my hand. "You were wrong to involve yourself in the ruckus with Amos. But I realize now that you were confused. You didn't understand."

I *had* understood though. Perfectly.

"Now the matter has been resolved. To my mind, the incident is closed." He smiled, as if to reassure me. He wouldn't punish me, he was saying.

But . . . *resolved?* Was that how he saw what had happened last night?

I nodded. For once I bit my tongue. But the anger was back again, in a fierce, burning wave.

Over the next week I watched them leave: on the *Elvina*, on the schooner *Crescent City*. These were sad processions, with the Celestials clutching children and worldly goods, disappearing at last into the vessels' holds.

The wagons had been taken to Edwards Corner, I learned—two miles east of Crescent City. The Chinese men, after scraping together what few possessions they could carry, had joined the women and children there. No burnings. No killings. As each San Francisco–bound ship came into harbor Mr. Hinkley drove a wagonload of Celestials up onto the dock, and the procession began.

I sat by the window, with the spyglass, and watched. For the most part I could not make out their faces from so far. But a body can, I discovered, discern misery at a distance—by a pair of hunched shoulders, by a down-turned head, by a slow and dragging gait.

Mama tried to lure me from the window with pie and hot cocoa. I refused. I could *feel* Papa's disapproving gaze warming the back of my head. But I didn't budge. Again I wondered, did he know about Sadie and me, the night of the eviction? Not likely. He wouldn't let *that* pass without punishment.

I searched long and hard for my China boy. I saw two who seemed his size, but they wore the wrong kind of hat.

The grandfather, though—I did see him, I was nearly certain. Two old men clambered down from the cart. They struggled to tote one lumpy bundle between them, shuffled together down the dock. One man was short and round and limping, the other skinny and stooped.

But if that *was* the grandfather . . . where was my China boy? Why didn't he help?

That first week Mama was home, Mary Connor came in four days to keep the household running. I soon felt myself again, but Mama took longer; she sat often to rest and bedded down early. It was agreed: I would stay home from school till the end of April to help. One day, when Papa was out, I saw Mama pouring a cup of the yellow green tea I'd seen at the hospital. "What kind of tea is that?" I asked her.

"It's something the doctor gave me. For . . . balance, he said."

"Balance?"

"It . . . lifts my spirits. Doctor says it's worked wonders, as to that."

"Is it . . . Chinese?"

Mama looked up sharp.

I rushed on. "Because if it is, won't you run out? With them gone?"

Mama put a lump of sugar in the tea, swished it with her spoon. She didn't look at me. "Doctor's laid in a good supply. And I'm scarcely needing it now."

"That's good," I said. But she hadn't denied it. It *must* be Chinese. A picture of the stooped old man in the herbalist's shop flashed into my mind.

"Liza? There's something else, isn't there?"

I shrugged.

"What? You can tell me. What is it?"

"Doesn't seem right. You drinking their tea to get well, then we run them out of town."

Mama turned away from me, gazed out the window. My words, when I heard them, sounded harsh. "I'm glad you have the tea, Mama," I said. "Real glad. But the other . . . doesn't seem right."

Mama took a sip of tea. Swallowed. Looked me square in the eye. "No," she said. "It doesn't."

"Does Papa know it's Chinese?"

She sighed. "I can't see any use in telling him. It would only stir him up." Mama reached out, clasped my hand. "Eliza, there are some things no amount of words can remedy."

Maybe so, I thought. But if nobody was willing to stir folks up, how would truth ever come out? How would things ever change?

Sadie came by every week to drop off schoolwork. She gave me news of the goings-on in town—how Mrs. Cuthbertson was feuding with Mrs. Somersby over what Mrs. Somersby had said about the Cuthbertsons' penny-pinching ways; how Robby Hinkley had dipped Hetty Overmeyer's braids in his inkwell at school. When I asked about the China shanties, she said they were empty, save for Mr. Plunkett, who had traipsed right in, taken over the washhouse, and raised prices by a penny a garment.

"Amos, he quit school," she said. "He's helping clear stumps over to the O'Brien place while his pa sets home and drinks."

"His papa . . . didn't get his job back?"

Sadie shook her head.

I couldn't help feeling sorry for Amos—a little.

"What about your papa?" I asked. "Is he glad the Celestials are gone?"

Sadie shrugged. "Job's safe. He's glad of that. But it ain't right, what those men done, Pa says. And other folks are saying the same. Not many. But some."

One day Sadie motioned me up to my bedroom. The moment we were inside, she said, soft and fast, "Yesterday Amos collared me after school. He said he has something of yours, but he wouldn't tell what—only said he found it on a boulder near the isthmus."

I felt my breath catch. "He wouldn't say at all?"

"I tried to make him tell, but—"

"What does he figure to do with it? Did he say that?"

"No. Just that if you want it, you can go fetch it. From him."

"Has he . . . does anyone else know . . . about that night? That we were *there?*"

"I don't reckon so. If Ma'd got wind of it, she'd of skinned me."

Amos. What did he have? And what would he do with it?

"Liza?" Sadie was looking at me, questioning. I wanted to tell her. I purely did. But Sadie would *do* something—that's just how she was. Like the day at the China shanties, when she *had* to look for my China boy. She'd go spying on Amos, or let it slip someway.

"I can't tell you about it," I said. "Not now. I will someday."

I could tell Sadie wanted to know more. I could see in her eyes that she was hurt. But she nodded, and we went on to speak of other things.

In scraps of spare time I began to read the Bible. Not just the old, familiar stories and admonitions against sin that Papa read to us of an evening, nor the comforting psalms that Mama loved. *The Lord is my shepherd. . . . Make a joyful noise . . . I will lift up mine eyes unto the hills . . .*

No, I was looking for passages about being kind to your neighbor. About how all men are brothers. I was looking for answers. How could God have let our baby die? Why did he ignore our prayers? I was looking for *proof.* How did we know that God truly existed? Surely I could find that in the Bible!

The night we walked to Sadie's house, Dr. Wilton had told me to be patient, to read through the whole Bible to find the shape of it.

That's the only way to puzzle it out, he said. So I started at the beginning but soon bogged down at the *begats*. The Bible repeated itself in places, and I soon discovered that Papa had left out parts of certain stories. The story of Abraham, for one. To save his own skin, Abraham lied—pretended his wife was his sister and just up and *gave* her to Pharaoh. *Concubine*, Papa had noted in his Bible.

"What's a concubine?" I asked Mama one day over the slap and gurgle of the churn.

"A concubine!" Mama looked up from her kneading. "My gracious! Where did you hear *that?*"

"In Papa's Bible."

"Oh! Well. A concubine is . . . a sinful woman."

"Sinful . . . how?"

"Just sinful, Eliza. That's all you need to know."

"But—"

"Would you set this bread to rise? There's a squall coming on, and I'd best fetch in the wash from the line."

I sighed.

Still, this was livelier matter than the passages Papa had marked. I read on, skipping around a bit.

Soon I began to doubt that I would find proof of God's existence. In olden times there were Heavenly Hosts and burning bushes and pillars of fire. Folks saw God, and his angels spoke directly with them. Or so the Bible claimed. A body couldn't *prove* it.

But then I wondered: Did other folks see God . . . today? Truly *see* him? Was I the only soul who couldn't?

"Mama," I asked another day, "have you ever seen God?"

She set her mending in her lap. "What do you mean, Eliza? *Seen God*, indeed!"

"I mean *seen* him. With your own eyes."

"That's not how you see God, dear. You see him in your heart. You hear him in your mind."

I had half hoped for a simple *yes*.

I began reading the newspaper, too. It said we were well rid of the curse of the Chinese evil. It said ours had been a peaceable eviction, that no one had been hurt. Only one Chinaman had come to bodily harm, the paper said—hit and knocked to the ground by a tap on the head with the butt end of a revolver.

I wondered how a *tap* could knock a body to the ground. I wondered—if the writer had seen the women and children dragged into the wagons, if he had heard their cries—how he could say that no one had been hurt.

And yet . . . life went on. The sedum bloomed; its sweet fragrance wafted in amongst the sea smells. The sun stayed out longer between squalls. One morning I heard something new from one of the near shoals. High, mewing sounds.

Harbor seal pups! I spent the better part of the morning on the rocks near the edge of the island, watching through the spyglass. So precious, they were, all velvet smoky gray with enormous, dark eyes—nuzzling their mamas or floundering about the shoal. As I watched, one of the seals flipped her pup into the water. He swam back, taking great gulps of air and wriggling like a fish—so eager, with the world so new.

It's odd how you can feel clenched up and angry at the world—but then some part of you stirs and stretches, starts to breathe. Without your permission. Without your trying, or even wanting it to happen.

I still worried about Amos—what he'd found, what he'd do. I worried he'd tell Papa I'd been out at the China shanties that night. Sometimes I thought about the China boy and those two old men—worried about what had become of them.

One Friday late in April, three weeks after

Mama had come home, I collected sand, shells, and seaweed and fetched them to the hospital. Under Dr. Wilton's magnifying glass the scatter of tan-colored sand sprang up to form cut jewels —rose and emerald, amber and jet. Each shell was a landscape unto itself, with high cliffs and dangerous scarps, with gentle dales and ancient, dried-up seabeds. A host of outlandish creatures patrolled the seaweed fronds.

"Secret world," I murmured.

"I've often thought that myself!" Dr. Wilton said. "That this world we know is supported by a web of things beyond the boundaries of what we can see and smell and hear. Secret worlds, as you put it. With a glass you can cross some thresholds—"

"Or you can walk across," I said. "When the tide lays bare *that* world, the one that's under water."

A slow smile crossed Dr. Wilton's face. "Yes," he said. "You *see* it, don't you?"

That night when I went out in the rain to shut Parthenia in her pen, I found her sniffing at the carpentry shop door. I called, but she didn't come. No surprise in *that*. It was only when I drew nearer that I noticed the door was ajar.

We never locked that door. But Papa always shut it when he left, slipped a dowel through the hasp.

"Parthenia! Come here!"

Just to spite me, she nudged the door open, vanished inside the shop. Heaven only knew what she would get into. I hastened up the path and stepped inside.

Dark. I couldn't see a thing. There was a musty smell, like wet wool, and something else I couldn't name. Then the beacon passed, swept a bright swath across the room. I found Parthenia, grasped her collar, and had begun to coax her toward the door when a rustling sound came from deep within the shop.

A raccoon, crossed over the isthmus at low tide? A possum?

I turned, peered into the darkness. As the light passed again I saw it: something stirring.

Something—*someone*—rising from a crouch to stand.

13

TOO KIND

At first I couldn't move. My body and my mind felt mired. Then I wanted to scream, but the sound wouldn't come up my throat. Parthenia lurched, slipped from my grasp. I whirled round to flee—but then, "Wait. Please. Wait."

A Chinese voice. I knew by the way he said *please*.

I turned back. I couldn't see him clearly—just the shape of him in the darkness at the far end of the shop. I stood peering into the gloom, breathing in the sweet fragrance of wood chips, the acrid tinge of turpentine, and the wet wool smell I'd noticed before. Now he moved a little forward; I shrank toward the door. At that moment the beacon swept past, lighting the planes of his face.

I knew him at once. The China boy.

Heathen. Papa's voice echoed in my mind, sparked a quick flicker of fear. What would he do to me? He must be angry, after what had happened. I ought to run, but . . .

"I no place stay," he said.

It took me a moment to fathom his meaning. *I have no place to stay.* With no blame, no anger, no whining. Just the unvarnished fact. And all at once I felt . . . ashamed. Ashamed of why he had no home to go to. I wondered why he hadn't gone on the ship with his grandfather, but my mouth wouldn't form the question.

"I stay one day. Maybe two. I no trouble."

There would be a world of trouble if Papa found him here.

"But why did you come *here?*" I said, then felt ashamed again. Where else could he go?

"Town, many people," he said. "No place hide. Island . . ."

Rain tapped on the roof. The beacon passed again, chased shadows across the shed. It caught the boy's dark eyes, intent upon me. Quickly he lowered his gaze.

Of course. He came here on account of *me*. Because he *knew* me, someway. Because he thought that I would help.

"Chinee," he said after a moment. "They force go . . . Frisco?"

It sounded like *Flisco* when he said it; he switched his *r*s and *l*s, as I had heard other Celestials do.

"You weren't there? You didn't see?"

"No. I . . . gone."

"Well, they did. Send them to San Francisco. But no one was . . ." *Hurt*, I was going to say. Like that liar of a newspaper writer. "Your grandfather . . . I saw him . . . board the ship."

"Grandfather?" He sat up straight, and his voice suddenly filled with warmth. "You see grandfather? You know him?"

"Someone . . . told me. Who he is. The herbalist. Is that right?"

The boy nodded eagerly. "How . . . how he . . ."

He didn't seem to be able to finish the question. But I could guess what he wanted to know. "He was . . . walking," I said carefully. "He seemed . . . well enough."

"I take boat Frisco! Find grandfather."

"No, you can't." He couldn't just sashay down the dock and board a ship, even if he had the

139

fare, which I doubted. No telling what would happen to him if he tried. "You need to pay for that," I said. "Do you have money?"

"I *walk* Frisco. No trouble *you*." Now he seemed offended.

"You can't walk to San Francisco! It's too far. Besides, there are folks who . . ." I stopped myself. *Who don't like Chinamen*, I was going to say. *Who might harm you*.

"I *walk*." The beacon passed again, whitewashed his face with light. There was a mulish set to this boy's jaw, I saw. He was wearing a black skullcap. I wondered what had become of his straw hat.

I peered back through the doorway, toward the house. Parthenia was grazing in the rain. The kitchen window was a square of light; I could see Mama moving about within. Up in the tower Papa gazed out to sea. I moved away from the doorway, into the shadows, thinking. . . .

It was one thing to take gifts from the boulder or to let Parthenia spoil Amos's fun. And even the night of the eviction . . . I'd only wanted to stay with Sadie. We hadn't interfered.

But *this*. This was different. If I hid him here, it'd be in pure *defiance* of Papa.

If only this boy had gone to San Francisco with the rest of them! The thought flashed through my mind, and I felt bad right off for thinking it. But still. If he *had*, I wouldn't be in this pickle.

Light again, then dark. There were hollows in his cheeks. He was thin, thinner than I remembered. Hungry, most like. Where had he been? Had anyone fed him?

Just this one night . . . I'd think of something. . . .

"I'll fetch you some victuals," I said. "I don't know if I can do it tonight. But in the morning I will. You'd best . . . you'd best not let my papa see you. Not yet. I'll speak with him. You needn't worry. But not yet. He's . . ." I stopped. I was babbling, talking too fast. Likely, he hadn't comprehended a word.

"Stay here until I return. Tomorrow morning, at the latest. I'll fetch victuals. Food. Do you understand?"

"Food," he said, and some of the starch seemed to go out of him. I could hear the hunger in his voice and saw that he was shivering.

"Yes! Wait for me until tomorrow. Don't set off for San . . . for Frisco. Not yet."

He ducked his head. "You too kind."

Too kind? I thought as I shut the door behind me. Someway this got my dander up. None of us had been too kind to this boy, to leave him hungry and cold and scared, hiding in Papa's carpentry shop. None of us had been near kind enough.

I couldn't get out again that night. Though Mama retired early, Papa was up and down between the supply closet and the lantern room. Impossible to leave.

But neither could I sleep. My mind rattled around like a loose cartwheel; my legs fidgeted and kicked until the bedclothes were all askew.

The China boy. Hiding out in our shed!

How could I get him food without it being missed? And this notion of walking to San Francisco—he didn't have a lick of sense! If Papa were willing, he could smuggle him off the island onto a boat. But he wouldn't. He was too upright to sneak. And the way he felt about *heathens* . . . And Mama—even when she took exception to Papa's views—would never defy him. Never go behind his back.

Still, the boy must leave, and soon. If Papa found him, he would be bound to report him to the Lighthouse Service. I knew the rule. *Permission will not be given by the keeper to any person to occupy any premises belonging to the*

Lighthouse Establishment. In case of trespass . . . make report without delay.

And *then* what would happen? Would the inspector arrest the boy? Put him in jail?

Or would Papa just evict him from the island? For the townsfolk to deal with. The Committee of Twenty-one.

What would *they* do?

Maybe just set him on a boat bound for where he wanted to go. *Frisco.* What would be amiss with that?

But maybe they wouldn't. Those miners . . . in Montana . . .

He had come here on account of *me.* I felt . . . responsible someway.

But I had a duty to Papa and Mama, too. A duty to be worthy of their trust.

Just before I drifted off to sleep, the answer came.

Dr. Wilton. *Soft on Chinamen*, Mrs. Calhoun had said. Surely *he* would help.

The kitchen was warm when I came downstairs, the cookstove ruddy and humming. Mama was setting out biscuits. She smiled and gave me two, "to sustain me," she said, while I milked Parthenia.

"One more?" I asked. She laughed, handing me a third, and speculated my leg must be hollow.

I felt bad, deceiving her.

Still, I thrust the biscuits into my apron pocket and, when Mama turned back to the stove, reached behind her and snatched a coffee mug from the cupboard.

It was chilly outside but not raining. Parthenia scrambled onto her milking stand when I arrived, eager for her oats. I fixed the bars of the stanchion around her neck and set to washing her udder. Of a brisk morning this was a pleasant task; her udder, soft and warm, thawed my numbed hands. But today I was in a hurry. Thinking to save time, I didn't tie her back leg to the milking stand. A mistake. No sooner had she finished her oats than she rolled her head, all huffy, then stepped in the milking pail.

"Oh . . . you . . . goat!"

I did not tarry as usual to scratch between her toes; she let out a long, protesting bleat. I set down the pail and dipped out a cupful of milk, then picked up Parthenia's blanket, shook it out, and tucked it under one arm. I hurried over the rise to the carpentry shop.

"Hello," I said, knocking softly at the door. Then I slipped inside.

Darkness still clung to the corners and floor, but the gray glow of dawn seeped in through the eastern windows. Papa's carpentry tools looked black against the walls where they hung; cans of whiting and paint and turpentine stood neat and straight on their shelves, like ranks of toy soldiers.

He's gone, I thought, and the sharp pang of disappointment surprised me.

But then I heard movement, and from beneath the workbench against the near wall the boy's head poked out.

"I have breakfast," I said. He clambered to his feet, said nothing. Maybe *breakfast* wasn't a word he understood. I set down the blanket, held up a biscuit and the milk. "Victuals. Food."

I could see him better now than I had the night before. His face *was* thin—too thin—and smudged with dirt. His pigtail, which had hung neat and glossy down his back when I saw him before, was now tangled, coming undone. His blue cotton jacket looked damp; it was stained and torn. A worn pair of leather boots stood beside him on the floor. His feet, I saw, were bloody, rubbed raw. The boy looked hungrily at the biscuit, but his eyes, when they moved to regard me, held nothing of greed, nothing of begging, nothing of wariness. They were grave, measuring.

He reached for the biscuit. It went down fast. So did the second and third.

Again I offered the mug. "Milk," I said.

He peered inside, then pulled back, wrinkling his nose.

"It's fresh from the goat!"

He looked down, seeming abashed.

"It's good for you!" And you look like you need it, I thought.

"No like," he said.

And Mrs. Calhoun thought *I* was finicky!

"You too kind," he added.

I shrugged, set the milk on the floor. "Not too kind," I mumbled. "Anyhow, you saved my goat. And . . ." Of a sudden I felt shy. "Did you . . . did you leave that bottle . . . for me? *Bottle? On the rock?*"

He hesitated, then nodded.

"And those candies? And the picture?" He looked puzzled. I pantomimed drawing. "Did you make that?"

"You like?"

"Yes!" I said. "It . . ." I swallowed against the lump that was rising in my throat, and the next words—which surprised me when they came—croaked out, whispery and hoarse. "It helped."

A hot flush was creeping up my cheeks. Our eyes locked for an instant; the boy looked down, scratched his ankle with a bare toe. Then, "You save hat." His hand moved to touch his skullcap, and he smiled a quick smile. "I lose two time. Very foolish boy."

I laughed, a quick letting-out of breath, and he smiled at me again.

"Well," I said. "Papa will be here soon. You'll have to hide somewhere for a spell." I pondered that for a moment. There were a number of places he might hide, but some would be difficult to explain. For now . . . hardly anyone went to the eastern side of the island, beyond the carpentry shed. There were plenty of bushes where he might hide, out of sight of both shed and shore.

"Bushes," I said, pointing out the window. "You hide. Understand?"

He looked troubled. "You . . . no tell father?"

"No. I . . . No. Not yet. But . . ."

"You father . . . no like I stay?"

I licked my lips. If I told him what Papa thought of the Celestials, he might leave right now. And I could scarcely blame him. "Don't

worry," I said. "I have a notion. To get you safely
. . . where you want to go. Frisco. But don't try
to walk there. Frisco is too far. And don't try to
get on a ship. It's not . . . safe. You wait. *Wait*."

"I find grandfather. Soon."

"Soon," I said. "But not yet. Not now."

"*Very* soon," he said, and his jaw had the mulish look again.

"Very soon," I agreed. "But for now, hide in
the bushes. Please."

He turned to gaze out the window. The soft
light caught the angles of his cheekbones, the
grim set of his mouth. He nodded, not looking at
me. "Bushes," he said. "Hide."

When the morning tide permitted, Papa ven-
tured to town on some errands and Mary
Connor came in to help Mama. I pilfered some
bread and jerky from the kitchen and slipped
down into the cellar for a couple of apples.
Likely they would not be missed this once. I
wrapped the food in a napkin and stowed it out
of sight of the house. Then I asked Mama if I
might go look at Dr. Wilton's microscope. She
admonished me not to pester the poor man but
waved me along.

I had planned, after fetching the napkin, to walk along the path for as far as it might be seen from the house and cut back up the slope to find the China boy. But the seashore was speckled with folks. It was Saturday morning and one of the lowest tides of the year—a prime day for finding mussels and butter clams, for scavenging shells and sea-polished stones. A prime day for seagulls, too; they mobbed the isthmus, screeching and diving.

I wavered, squinting up toward the bushes on the slope behind the shed. No sign of the boy. Well. He *wouldn't* have left, I didn't reckon. Best not to draw notice to myself, thrashing about in the bushes. I'd come back later, after I'd spoken with Dr. Wilton, when there was less chance of being seen.

I caught him just as he was stepping into his buggy. "What is it, Eliza?" he asked. "I'm in a bit of a rush. Mrs. Sawyer's time is come."

Her baby. I felt a stab of jealousy but pushed right through. "I . . . need help," I said. "Not for me, but—"

"Come along then," he said. "We can talk on the way."

Thank heaven I'd come in time! I tossed the napkin with the food into the buggy, gathered my skirts, and climbed in after, certain that all would be well.

The doctor urged his graying mare, Daisy, to a halfhearted trot. I cut my story to bare bones—how the China boy had saved Parthenia, how I'd found him in the shed.

"You've told your folks none of this?" he asked.

"No. Papa—"

He held up a hand. "I know. But you must tell him."

"But—"

"You must. I'd go with you now—we could speak with him together—but Mrs. Sawyer . . ." We jolted around the corner onto B Street; Dr. Wilton snapped the reins in a foredoomed effort to get Daisy to pick up the pace. "Likely nothing so ill will befall the boy," he said. "Your papa surely will do him no harm, just put him on a ship bound for San Francisco."

"But I thought *you* would take him in. Tonight, at ebb tide. I could tell him where to go. . . ."

The doctor was shaking his head. "I won't conspire with you behind your father's back, Eliza."

My hopes, so high just a moment before, seemed to dry up and sink within me. Things were darkening, tottering. "Papa won't let him stay on the island, even just until the next ship comes. The Lighthouse Service is particular about that, and there's already a blot on Papa's record." Because of *me*, I thought. "Papa will turn him over to someone else . . . likely not you. . . ."

"Likely not," the doctor agreed.

"The boy could go to jail! Or they might take him out to Edwards Corner, like before. They might *harm* him—folks are that riled. And he's starving; he's gone thin as a rail. And . . ." A new worry struck me. "Even if they did take him to San Francisco, how would he find his grandfather? It's a big city. He might *never* find him!"

"Whoa, Eliza. Simmer down. First of all, if he's truly starved, your father might well entrust him to me for medical care. As to San Francisco, the Chinese have organizations. Tongs. If he finds someone from the right tong—"

"But what if he doesn't!"

The doctor furrowed his brow. "You said he hopes to find his grandfather?"

"Yes. That old man . . . the herbalist."

Dr. Wilton looked at me sharply. "Wah Lin?"

"He's the herbalist?"

"And a thumping fine one too. Your mother —

well, never mind that. Wah Lin told me he had a grandson. Likes to draw."

"That's the one!"

"How did he escape being evicted with the rest?"

"I . . . don't know."

"Where's he been these weeks past? Is there a father somewhere? Wah Lin's son?"

"I don't know." I had forgotten to ask.

"What did you say his name was?"

His name. I hadn't even asked his name. *The China boy*—that was how I had thought of him. As if he weren't quite a real person, with a real name.

"I don't know," I said miserably.

The doctor hauled back on the reins; Daisy quit pretending to trot and slowed to a laggardly walk. And Mr. Sawyer was hastening toward us down the path from their home. "There you are, Doctor! Come in!"

Dr. Wilton turned to me. "I'll cogitate on this. I'm sure something can be worked out. But promise me you'll tell your folks as soon as you get home. *Promise.*"

I shook my head. "I can't." And before the doctor had a chance to stop me, I snatched up the bundle of food, jumped down from the buggy, and set off running for home.

14

WAH CHUNG

By the time I reached the isthmus, the tide was well on the rise. The wind had picked up; it lifted foam off the breakers, swept it into curling white combs. A patchwork of sullen clouds skimmed across the sky, and a line of dark rimmed the far horizon.

Storm coming, looked like.

What few scavengers who remained had moved northways, along the shore; the isthmus was deserted.

When I gained the island, I left the path and cut through the sedum, looking for the boy. I glanced at the tower. No Papa. I hoped he wasn't in the shop.

But then . . . A banging noise. And shouting.

I stumbled up the hill and, rounding the corner of the shed, spied Amos Tyler—shoulder to the door, trying to force it open.

"Amos! What in tarnation! Stop that right now!"

"I got a Chinaman trapped in your shop! I seen him hiding in the bushes. Chased him here. He got both doors blocked. You best go fetch your pa."

I swallowed. "Get you gone from here, Amos! You're trespassing!"

"*I'm* trespassing! And the Chinaman ain't?" He cocked his head to one side, like something had just occurred to him. "You're hiding him! I wager the keeper don't even know."

Heat flooded my face. "The doings on this island are no concern of yours. You're trespassing."

"I ain't trespassing. I come to show you *this*. I think your pa will thank me for it." He drew something from the pocket of his trousers: a small red tin with Chinese figures lettered in gold upon it. He opened it up. Inside, a folded sheet of rice paper.

"I wager you know where I found it."

"How would I know that?" I said, trying to squeeze the fear out of my voice.

"I seen you there once, over to the tall boulder by shore. I'd a mind to check time to time, see what was so confounded curious-making. You want to know what's writ here?" He tapped the paper.

I grabbed for it. He held it up, beyond my reach. I jumped. He swung round; his elbow smashed into my nose. It blinded me—the pain, and an upwelling of rage. Tears sprang into my eyes; something warm was flowing over my mouth.

Amos stared—almost frightened-seeming. "I didn't mean . . ." he said.

The fiercest part of the pain had begun to ebb, leaving a throbbing in my face, a tingling sting in my nose. I wiped my mouth with the back of my hand—something salty there—then gaped down at the thick smear of blood. I turned to Amos. "You're trespassing," I said, stone-cold. "If Papa finds you did *this* to me, he'll skin you alive."

"He'll skin *you* if he finds *him* here." Amos jerked his head toward the shop.

"He'll skin you first."

Amos wavered. His eyes flicked toward my bloody hand. "This ain't the end of it," he said, then turned and made for shore.

I checked the house again—no one in the tower, no one in the windows—then moved to where the oil shed hid me from view. I squatted, wiped my bloody hand on a clump of grass, wiped my face again.

A grinding, scraping noise inside the shop. In a moment the door opened a crack. The China boy peered both ways, then ran to me, knelt beside me.

"You hurt?" he asked.

"It's . . . better," I said. My nose tingled and throbbed, but the worst of the pain had gone.

"You do this." The boy tipped his head back, pinched the bridge of his nose.

I wiped off more blood.

"Stop blood," he said. "You do this."

Doubtful, I did what he had showed me. Blood streamed down my throat; I swallowed it. A little sob came back up, a strange, gurgling sound, and now my eyes were leaking too.

"I look boy," he said. "Back soon." I watched out of the corner of my eye until he disappeared from sight.

In a moment, when he returned, the bleeding seemed mostly to have stopped. I lowered my head, wiped my nose again, wiped my eyes.

"Is he gone?" I asked.

"Yes. Boy gone."

"Certain sure? You saw him?"

He nodded. "He walk . . . road."

With luck, Amos wouldn't return before the tide flooded the isthmus. "We'd best not stay here now," I said. I didn't know where Papa was. Not anyplace near, or he'd have come running. But he might come near soon.

"Hide bushes?"

"No. I know a better place."

Though our island was small, it had many secret places. When I was younger, I would have bread-crumb parties for birds behind the cisterns. Or make tents with sticks and blankets on the far side of the vegetable garden fence. Or crouch unseen against the leeward wall of the carpentry shop, listening to Papa work. Papa hummed while he worked—out of tune.

When I grew older, I explored the rocky out-crops at the island's edge.

There were certain places on the rocks where you couldn't be seen from anywhere else on the island—not even from the tower. I used to creep from secret place to secret place, pretending to be an Indian scout.

Now I picked up the food bundle and led the boy along one of my old Indian trails—behind the carpentry shed, down the slope to the barren rim of the island, over and around the clustered boulders to a tiny, rocky nook on the northwest side. Here, we were well hid and could shelter from the rising wind, from the spatters of rain that had begun to fall. Papa and Mama seldom came near here, and the sea would mute our voices.

I set down the bundle, then knelt, scooped up water from a passing swell. I rinsed the blood off my hands, tried to wash it from my face and apron.

"Is it gone?" I asked softly, pointing at my face. "The blood?"

He scrubbed a forefinger across his upper lip. I echoed the motion. Then he was taking off his blue cotton jacket, holding it out to me. "No," I said, "I—"

"Many stain," he said. "More stain no matter."

I was still shaking my head when he took the end of a sleeve and gently daubed under my nose. I wanted to pull away but forced myself to hold still. The jacket smelled peculiar—of incense, maybe. And sweat. Of sawdust and of smoke. Not unpleasant. He leaned back. "Blood gone," he said.

Up close, in full daylight, his face looked the

color of weak tea. He must have washed; it was perfectly clean. His eyes, though still strange-seeming, had a warm gleam in them. Like Sadie's eyes. Like a friend.

How could I tell him what a muddle I'd made of things? That I'd prattled to the doctor about him, and *he* would almost certainly tell Papa. And Amos . . . had he seen the boy from shore? Was that how he'd known he was here? I sighed. Well, no matter. He *would* talk . . . to someone. Was likely doing so now.

The boy was eyeing the napkin. I handed it to him; the bread and meat were gone in a flash, and half of the first apple. *If he's truly starved, your father might well entrust him to me.* But I couldn't wait for that, for the doctor to come. He wouldn't, tonight. But someone might. Amos, or someone he'd told. So I would steal out of the house, take the boy to Dr. Wilton the moment the isthmus came clear. Surely he wouldn't turn him away.

And Papa . . . Well. I'd tell him when it was done. Something curdled within me when I thought on that. I didn't want to deceive him. It was wrong, I knew. And yet, this boy . . .

This boy. "What is your name?" I asked. Then,

hearing the loud, ill-manneredness of the question, I stood and looked about to make certain no one was near, and added, "I'm Eliza. Eliza Jane McCully."

He swallowed a bite of apple. "I name Wah Chung."

Wah Chung. "Pleased to know you."

"Please know you."

"Wah Chung, did you leave me . . . a box?"

He looked at me, uncomprehending.

"A metal tin? Red with gold letters?"

Now he nodded, smiled. "For you. Tin. Picture."

"Picture?"

"Yes. You goat."

I must have looked blank, because his face suddenly fell. "Oh," he said, sounding disappointed. "You no see it goat."

"I . . . never saw it. I . . ." It would take too long to explain. "There was no writing?" I asked.

He shook his head.

So Amos had been bluffing about that. Still, the picture. *Parthenia.* After what had happened the day of the dinner bell, Amos might explain it so's to make it look bad. Like I'd been in cahoots someway.

"Wah Chung, where were you? While they

were . . . when the other Chinese folks . . . left town?"

"I gone. Grandfather send me. Fetch father."

"Your father. Where is he?"

"Winchuck River. He cook. Ranch. But I . . . lost. Come home."

His father? A cook, on a ranch?

All at once I was seized by an urge to know everything about Wah Chung—how he had survived his journey to this country, how his father had come to be a cook on the Winchuck River, why they had left China, what loved ones they had left behind. Who had taught Wah Chung how to stop a nosebleed? Where had he learned to draw? I was afraid I would offend him, prying, but it didn't take much—just a question or two more—to get him started. After that I had little need of asking. From time to time I stood and looked about, to make certain no one was near. Often I could scarcely understand him—his halting, mangled speech. But he seemed to know a lot of words.

Something was opening up between us—like a parting of waters, like a gap in the clouds—and through it I caught glimpses of another world across the sea. Of tall mountains and green fields. Of drought, of hunger and dust. Of two younger sisters—one sprightly and one sweet—and a toddling baby brother. Of a mother, alone, now, with the little ones. With only the earnings sent from this land to sustain them.

Wah Chung's throat stopped up when he spoke of his mother. He swallowed, went on.

There was something about a ship then, a voyage with his father to San Francisco. There was something about a man Wah Chung had met there, a man who made his living by painting . . . on crockery? On screens? Wah Chung, I gathered, had always loved to draw. Had drawn with sticks in the dirt. Had drawn on flat stones with fingers dipped in mud. This San Francisco man had given him a brush, a bottle of ink, and hope of someday living there. Of working for—or maybe *with?*—the man. The ink was gone now. Wah Chung still clung to the brush—and the hope.

The tide had come in, had covered the isthmus. The western horizon was dark. Storm coming. A faint sound of hammering came from the carpentry shop. Mama would expect me soon, I knew, to help with the midday meal. But I didn't want to leave, not just yet. "How did you come *here?*" I asked. "To Crescent City?"

There were more, shorter voyages, by land and by sea—some back-and-forthings I did not quite understand—with Wah Chung's grandfather ending in Crescent City, Wah Chung and his father on the ranch. Word came to them that the grandfather was ill. When two Chinamen they knew headed south to work in the lumber camps near Crescent City, Wah Chung went with them, to tend to his grandfather.

"Grandfather heal," Wah Chung said. "But . . . trouble, Crescent City. He send me fetch father. Father can help."

"You went alone?" I asked. "On foot?"

"Grandfather friend give . . . mule. Man steal. I lost. Come back. Grandfather gone."

Wah Chung picked at a patch of lichen. A raindrop pelted my nose.

"I'm sorry," I said.

Wah Chung shook his head. "No fault you. *I* fault."

"No! You did all you could."

Wah Chung looked up. His eyes were fierce. "I bad leave grandfather. He send me away . . . save *me*. No time fetch father. Grandfather know. *I* know."

A wave slapped against the rocks and hissed,

retreating. Wah Chung looked out to sea. "I *find* him," he said. "I *walk*."

"I . . . have another notion. Will you listen? Tell me what you think?"

He hesitated, nodded.

"I can come for you tonight. Or if this storm is bad, tomorrow. I can take you to someone . . . you can trust."

"Not . . . keeper. Not you father."

He must have understood some of what Amos and I had said. "No. Not him. But there is someone." I *hoped*.

He gave me an open, searching look, like he was trying to read my thoughts, like he was trying to read *me*. At last he nodded. He trusted me —which someway made it worse. Who knew but what a kindly teamster might have happened upon him walking, might have taken him to San Francisco? Who was I to put him at the mercy of my feeble plan?

A volley of raindrops pelted down on my bonnet; I shivered. Dread was closing round my heart.

I feared for this boy, Wah Chung.

15

STORM

I had thought to steal upstairs, inspect my face in the mirror before anyone could lay eyes on it, then run down and help with dinner. But Mama, setting the table in the sitting room, saw the bruise right off.

"Liza!" she said. She dropped the napkins, hastened toward me, brushed her finger beneath my left eye. "How did you come by this?"

Behind me I heard Papa enter the room. "I . . . I bumped into something." They were staring at me now—Mama and Papa. Puzzled.

"Uh, the gate to Parthenia's pen. I wasn't looking. I just . . . bumped into it."

"You're not feeling poorly are you, dear?" Mama asked. "Maybe you ought to—"

"No! I . . . I feel fine. I just wasn't . . . I was in a hurry and . . ." I shrugged.

"You'd best pump some cold water onto a cloth and put it on that eye," Papa said.

Between the creaks and glugs of pumping I could hear them murmuring in the sitting room. My lie hung in the air, like smoke.

Later that afternoon the ocean turned sickly green and the birds disappeared. Papa ceased with his record-keeping work and climbed up into the tower. I followed him there, found him gazing out to sea. Black clouds were boiling up over the edge of the earth and spilling across the sky.

"It's bad?" I asked.

"A weather breeder." He glanced at me, then turned back to brood upon the sea. "I'm fixing to board up the windows. You know what to do."

Storm duty: Fetch in wood for the stove. Help Papa with stacking boards. Set out extra feed for Parthenia and tether her to her shed.

I went right to work but couldn't be easy until Papa had returned from the carpentry shop with his first load of boards and I could see from his face that he'd found nothing amiss. I told myself that Wah Chung would fare well enough. Surely, once the storm arrived, he would shelter in the shop. It hunkered low on the island, east of the house. Unlike the privy, which had been lost many times to storms, the shop had never come to much harm.

As to my plan . . . If the storm hampered my crossing the isthmus with Wah Chung, it would prevent Amos as well. Tomorrow I'd fetch the doctor.

Come suppertime the storm had swallowed up the western sky. I fetched Papa's plate to him in the tower. Swells as large as hills came smoking in toward shore; foam lay like a white lace tablecloth spread across the water. Though the sun wouldn't set for an hour, Papa was lighting the beacon. "Set the victuals in the service room, Eliza," he said. "I'll get to them when I can."

I supped downstairs with Mama, washed the dishes, wiped down the sink. Though the thick stone walls muted the wind sounds, we could hear deep, muffled booms and feel faint tremblings underfoot when breakers hit the rocks. Soon as the coffee was done, I offered to take it up. I felt drawn into the tower, like I was tugged by the force of the moon.

The heat from the thick ceramic cup warmed my hands as I made my way up the stairs. I had done this for years, fetched Papa coffee during storms. I breathed in the bitter-rich smell, felt the steam warm my face. Above me I could hear the wind battering and howling. I could hear the thundering of waves, and rain pelting the glass like handfuls of flung stones.

Papa seemed grateful for the coffee. To the east, light seeped palely through the clouds. The tops of fir trees pitched and swayed. In the bea-con's spokes I saw fishing boats, anchored in the harbor, thrashing like hooked salmon. The lace tablecloth had vanished; the sea had gone pure churning white with foam. No one would cross the isthmus this night.

Footsteps on the stairs. When I looked down through the opening to the service room, Mama held up two mugs. I knelt to take them, my mouth watering at the whiff of hot cocoa. We stood beside Papa, watching the storm, listening. The din made talking hard, but we had no need of talk. My face, still aching some, tingled in the cold air. But the bull's-eyes warmed my back as they passed, and the cocoa warmed my insides.

I purely gloried in watching storms—loved

the raw power of them, loved standing at the edge of something huge and wild and raging. And yet here, in the circle hollowed out by the lantern room, I felt oddly *still*. Companionable. Safe.

Boom! Spume burst up from the rocks; a stream of foam crashed against a lantern pane, rattling the glass. *Wah Chung*. I glanced back toward the carpentry shed—still intact—and felt a small stirring of fear.

There is a sound that comes during storms at the lighthouse. Not the howling of the wind— something else. It starts as a growl, way back low in the throat, then builds to a deep, animal roar.

As the storm worsened, the sound began to shiver in the lantern panes; it began to rumble in the floor; it began to hum inside my bones. When big waves hit, the whole of the lantern room quaked. Air moved strangely through the tower, changed the pressure someway. Like it was a live thing. Like it was breathing.

I fetched the caulk, tried to silence the chattering glass. In vain. Rain ran down it in rivers, and wave after wave spewed froth tower-high. By the light of the beacon I saw seaweed hanging off the keeper's walk.

Mama returned downstairs. I ferried to and from the kitchen, fetching more coffee and, when it was done, a plateful of fresh spice cake. The waves from the northwest were truly alarming now, looming higher and higher, shouldering nearer and nearer to the house, to the carpentry shop.

The house would hold, I was certain of that. And Parthenia—her tiny, three-sided shed lay on the southeast of the island, in the lee of the storm. But the carpentry shop . . .

I pictured Wah Chung, huddled there. He trusted me. . . .

As I watched, a breaker crashed against the privy. In the next spoke of light it was flotsam, a mess of sticks.

"The privy!" I called to Papa. "It's gone."

He groaned.

The carpentry shop—undamaged, so far as I could tell. But the *stillness* I had felt before . . . had begun to come unraveled.

I didn't see the big wave until it was too late to do anything but shout. It broke against the rocks, and then a towering plume of white water slammed into the glass on the northwest side of the tower. One of the panes bulged inward; I gaped in frozen horror as cracks spiderwebbed across it. I flung myself down the ladder just as bedlam broke out—shattering glass, spewing water, hissing steam. Dark, of a sudden. The beacon—dark.

Papa called down to me, "Eliza! Are you hurt?"

I didn't feel hurt. Wet, but not hurt. Scared, but not hurt. There was water on the floor. And glass. It crunched beneath my feet.

"No. Are you?"

"Fetch me a new chimney, and the hammer and nails. And boards! Fetch me some boards! Then get yourself some gloves and start clearing away the glass. And the mop. And—"

"Fire!" Mama's voice, coming from below. "Kitchen's afire! *Fire!*"

Before I could stir myself, Papa was down the ladder, pushing past me, pounding down the stairs.

There was a bright orange light in the kitchen, and the air pulsed with heat. Crackling flames leaped from the curtains, from the outer wall. Through the black smoke I could see the cookstove, red-hot. There was a hole in the ceiling where the stovepipe used to be and water slicked across the floors. And beyond the fallen stovepipe . . . Mama and Papa. Papa pumping water from the cistern pump. Mama flinging it on the flames.

That wave must have knocked off the stovepipe. Flying sparks must have kindled the fire.

Boom. A column of water poured down through the roof hole, flooded the kitchen, lapped across the sitting room floor. A deafening hiss: steam and smoke erupted in a billowing cloud; I couldn't see a thing. But in a moment it thinned, and Mama and Papa, sooty and drenched, appeared at the door.

"Fire's out," Papa said. "Rose, you salvage what you can between waves. Eliza, swab the decks here, then come up to help in the tower." He seized an armload of boards, started for the stairwell, then turned back.

"Go easy, Rose. *You* mean more to us than any of this."

Mama set to salvaging, but I couldn't budge. Smoke hovered in the sitting room, blackening the ceiling, the tops of the lace curtains. Water seeped across the floor, darkening the blue rag rug. In the kitchen the cookstove had cooled to black, but a stale, burnt odor filled my nose.

This had never happened before. We'd had bad storms, lost the privy, lost lantern panes. But never this. The sea had breached the roof, had come inside the house.

Anything could happen.

And the carpentry shed. Not safe . . . Not after this.

Slowly I began to move.

Don't think on it, I told myself as I shrugged into my slicker and pulled on my boots. You're going to do this. But you don't have to think.

The front door was on the southeast side of the house, sheltered from the worst of the storm. I stepped outside before I had a chance to change my mind. The sound of the storm, muffled inside by the thick granite walls, swelled up and beat against me: a screaming of wind, the crash and hiss of waves. Rain lashed at my face; the ground quaked with the concussion of pounding water.

I moved in the direction of the oil shed, staying in the lee of the house for as long as I might. It was dark, hard to see, except when the beacon's spokes passed—bright silver ribbons full of sea spume and rain.

Papa had got it lit. He *always* got it lit.

Boom. In the next pass of the beacon I saw that

the sea was running on the land. Spray poured down on me from clear over the house. A river ran past, between the oil shed and the house.

We should have built an ark.

I waited for the water to drain off, then stepped away from the house. A screaming blast of wind and rain struck me, knocked me back against the house. I leaned into it, pushed all my weight against it. *Boom.* Gouts of salt spray pelted my face, hard as hail. Water surged about my knees, then ebbed again.

The oil shed. I rested in the lee of it, took stock. Too chancy to try the carpentry shop door, on the northwest side of the building. Better to keep south, go to the window on the end.

Into the wind again. Up a little rise, then down. I pounded on the window of the shop. "Wah Chung! Open up! Wah Chung!"

There he was, on the other side of the glass. The sash slid partway up.

"Come *now*," I said, nearly shouting in his ear. "To the house!"

He hesitated. Then, "You father. Take me . . . other men."

"It isn't safe! You *have* to come."

"I stay."

"Don't be stubborn, Wah Chung. Now, *come*. Please!"

"You give word?" Wah Chung asked. "Men no take me?"

How could I give my word?

How could I *not?*

Another boom. The shop shook like it was seized with palsy. I heard shattering glass, and a flood of seawater gushed past my boots. "Yes," I said. "Now, *come*."

Wah Chung pushed open the window and climbed out.

It was harder, going back. The wind, angled more against us, battered at me, dragged at my sodden skirts. A sudden gust flung me backward; I slammed into a boulder. Wah Chung thumped back beside me. The air was full of water—rain and sea. Wah Chung shouted something, then pushed away, went hunching toward the oil shed. I peeled myself off the rock, crouched behind him until the wind let up in the lee of the shed.

We rested there a moment, then set off for the house. A wave seethed over the island above my knees. I heaved myself against the press of water and wind.

Something moving, just ahead, very near the house. Then a bleat, so full of indignation that I almost wanted to laugh. Parthenia. She stumbled toward me, bumped her head against my stomach, bleated again. Well. I couldn't leave her here. I grabbed her collar, hauled her into the lee of the house. She lurched toward the front door; my toe jammed into a rock and I went flying, hit down kneefirst on something sharp, something that *hurt*.

Parthenia. Where had she gone?

When I saw her again, in a shaft of beacon light, it seemed a scrap of an old dream. Because Wah Chung was holding her in his arms, like the first time I'd met him.

Slowly I clambered to my feet. I mounted the steps to the front stoop, opened the door, motioned to Wah Chung.

"After you," I said.

16

IT WOULD TAINT US

Mama saw us first.

She was backing out of the kitchen, toting an armful of soggy provisions. She shut the kitchen door and, "Oh there you are, Eliza," she said, beginning to turn. "I thought you were setting to—"

Her glance snagged on Wah Chung, and I watched her face change, watched her eyes pass through startlement to a look I couldn't fathom, a look somewhere between pity and wonder.

Parthenia kicked hard, squirmed out of Wah Chung's arms, and made for the flowers on the side table. When she produced a hill of black pellets on the floor, Mama dropped the provisions and ran to seize the goat's collar. "Eliza, remove your boots and take Parthenia to the cellar," she said. "Young man—"

"His name is Wah Chung," I said. "He was . . . he has no place to stay."

Mama straightened as far as she could without turning loose of Parthenia. She pushed a strand of hair out of her eyes, seemed to gather herself together. "Wah Chung," she said. "I'm Rose McCully. Pleased to make your acquaintance."

Wasn't that just Mama all over? Sooty and drenched, the house flooded and burned, a goat in her sitting room—and still all over a *lady*.

"But . . ." Mama did look a bit dazed. "How did you come here, Wah Chung? In this storm?"

"I found him last night," I said, "in the carpentry shop. I fed him. I—"

A wave boomed against the house; I could hear water pelting down in the kitchen. Mama turned her wondering gaze upon me.

Footsteps on the stairs. "Eliza, where are you? I need—"

When he caught sight of Wah Chung, Papa's jaw went slack.

"James," Mama said in a voice that brooked

no interruption, "this is Wah Chung. Wah Chung, Captain McCully."

Wah Chung bowed a little bow. Papa's jaw snapped shut. Then, "Where in tarnation did he—"

Mama broke in. "He's but a boy, James. A boy who needs our help."

Papa's brows knit together. "He's a—"

"A *boy*. He's but a *boy*."

Parthenia let out a querulous bleat. "The beacon needs tending, James," Mama said. "Eliza'll come in a moment."

Papa turned to her, looked back at Wah Chung, and then, to my astonishment, obeyed.

Mama sorted through the calamity one mishap at a time. She directed Wah Chung to her rocking chair, then, laying eyes on my stocking—torn and soaked with blood—commanded me to sit on the floor. She tethered Parthenia to a door latch, swept up her droppings, gave her a ruined straw basket to chew on, and threatened dire consequences if she should even contemplate escape. Then she put me on notice not to budge while she fetched what was needful from upstairs.

I looked at Wah Chung, wanting to reassure him but not knowing how. Wind whistled faintly in the tower; raindrops plinked against the fallen stovepipe in the kitchen. He caught my eye, smiled faintly, cleared his throat. I was afraid he would ask what Papa was going to do. Instead he motioned to my stocking. "You have hurt?" he asked.

I tucked my foot under my skirt and shrugged. "A little. My toe. My knee."

A wave boomed against the house; water lapped into the sitting room from beneath the kitchen door. "Grandfather," Wah Chung said, "he know fix hurt. He have . . . medicine." He stopped. I nodded, not knowing what to say. And in my mind I saw his grandfather—who had medicine, who knew how to fix hurt—herded like a cow onto that wagon.

Mama came downstairs and sent Wah Chung— with a folded stack of Papa's clothing—to the spare room to change. She washed my knee as best she could, though she couldn't get deep enough to scour out all the sand. I gritted my teeth against the pain; I didn't want Wah Chung to hear me cry. She poured on boric acid, then stanched the bleeding with cornstarch, holding the gash together and binding it with strips of linen. "You ought to have a stitch," she said, "but I reckon this will do."

Papa didn't speak to me all the rest of that night. I heard him from time to time, calling Mama up to help. I saw him but once, when he came down intending to nail boards over the hole where the stovepipe had been.

"Who did this?" he demanded when he saw that the job had been done.

"Wah Chung," Mama said, real soft.

Papa turned to watch Wah Chung lugging a bag of potatoes into the sitting room. He looked hard at the nailed-up boards, like he was inspecting.

"He's helping, James," Mama said. "Heaven knows we need it."

Papa grunted, headed toward the stairs.

"Papa?" I said.

He stopped, his back to me, then went through the door and shut it. Without a word. Without a look.

I bore down on the mop, tears filling my eyes. There was a hole in my heart, a place once filled with the certainty of Papa's love.

Wah Chung helped move foodstuffs into a dry corner of the sitting room, insisting Mama not lift too much. He looked an oddity in Papa's clothes—trouser legs and sleeves heavy with the weight of rolled-up cloth.

The heap of provisions grew: burlap bags of potatoes, beans, split pease, and onions; the big iron kettle; crates of crockery, pots, and pans; jars of tomatoes, corn, pickles, and preserves; a pail of lard; tins of molasses, baking powder, and cocoa. But all the rice had been burned beyond saving, and the cornmeal and flour had turned to paste.

After a time the booming waves grew fainter, farther between. Soon the sitting room floor was nearly dry; Mama and I wrung out the rag rugs as best we could, then hung them up in the cellar.

At last, long past bedtime, when the storm had well subsided, we halted for the night. Mama dug through the heap of provisions and offered Wah Chung and me jerky and ginger-snaps. She was too kind, Wah Chung said, but made short shrift of her offerings—down to the last crumb. Then Mama packed him off to the spare room and admonished him to get some rest.

But she wasn't through with me. Just as I slipped beneath the covers I heard her footsteps creaking up the stairs.

"Eliza?"

She came inside, settled herself at the foot of my bed. "Now, tell me," she said, "about Wah Chung."

I woke to the sound of hammering. Early-morning sunshine poured through the chink between my curtains and laid a yellow stripe across my quilt. I drew the curtains aside. Steam rose in clouds from the wet shingles. Papa had rigged a new chimney for the cookstove from a piece of metal pipe; it puffed smoke in a gentle breeze.

The night before, I had told Mama every-thing—about how Wah Chung had saved Parthenia, about the gifts left on the rock, about yesterday's talk with Dr. Wilton, about find-ing Wah Chung in the shed. I told about Amos as well, but not about my black eye. He hadn't intended that.

"What will Papa do?" I'd asked. "I gave my word we wouldn't turn him over to anyone . . . like Amos. Or the Committee of Twenty-one."

Mama had sighed. "You had no right to make that promise. Your papa will decide. Still, I'll try to persuade him to take Wah Chung to Dr. Wilton."

But persuading Papa . . . that was no trifling task.

And what, I wondered, would Papa do with *me?*

The sitting room looked like a mercantile shop—a mighty cluttered one. Kettles, milk pans, pitchers, plates, cups, ladles, bowls, rolling pin, coffee grinder, churn. Wah Chung came through the front door toting some boards across to the kitchen. He smiled shyly.

"G'morning, Liza," Mama said, peering out of the kitchen. "How does that knee of yours? How does your eye?"

"Better. My knee's a mite stiff. But Parthenia . . . I'm late milking her. . . ."

"She's out in the shed. Best get to it."

I wanted to ask what had been decided about Wah Chung, but I couldn't think how to put my tongue to the question. It would be unmannerly, with him right there with us. I wondered if she had spoken to him of it. Perhaps it had been happily settled?

And Papa . . . how angry was he? Would he ever speak to me again?

When I returned from milking, I helped Mama and Wah Chung wash dishes and utensils, helped sift through the foodstuffs partly ruined by fire or smoke or water to salvage what lay unharmed. In the light of day the view of the kitchen was heartbreaking. Though the gaps in the wall had been patched over with boards, dust and bits of crumbling wood drifted down from the blackened roof beams, and the whole of it reeked of smoke. Saddest of all were the remnants of Mama's cheery touches: a scorched flower-print dishcloth, the charred remains of the pink gingham curtains over the sink.

Papa stayed outdoors. He worked on the roof for a spell, then disappeared within the carpentry shop. That building stood intact—not washed out to sea. Scarcely harmed at all, save for a window or two.

What a fine kettle of fish I'd landed us in! If only I'd kept my head and left Wah Chung there during the storm. I'd been a pure fool!

Well. *If onlys* don't cut kindling. But soon—as soon as the tide permitted—I would slip out and fetch the doctor.

I was scrubbing smoke from the churn when a knock came at the door. That took us by surprise. The sea was still high—well above the tide rocks. Whoever was come had taken his life in his hands.

Mama shooed Wah Chung into the spare bedroom; I started for the door. The doctor. It *must* be the doctor. Mama's voice brought me up sharp. "*I'll* get it, Eliza. You stand back."

The door swung open. Not the doctor.

Amos Tyler and his father.

My heart shrank until it was a hard little stone inside my chest. I watched the drips and runnels coming off their trousers and boots, watched the growing puddle on the stoop.

"Good day, Mrs. McCully," Mr. Tyler said. "Is the keeper at home?" He took off his cap, crumpled it in a bear-sized paw. His ears were huge and meaty. He glanced at Amos—"Take that off," he said—and swatted the cap from his son's head. Amos scrambled to retrieve it. His face had gone red. He didn't meet my eyes.

"He's working in the shop," Mama said. "Liza, go fetch your father." She turned a blinding smile on Mr. Tyler. "I'd invite you in, but the house is in no fit state. The storm breached the roof and we had a fire in the kitchen. But would you care for a cup of tea? I'll set a blanket on the stoop; we can—"

"Thank you kindly, but we ain't come to tea. Eliza," he said, nodding a solemn greeting as I drew near the door. His eyes fixed on mine, and I remembered the bruise, wondered what Amos had told him.

Then I lit out for the shop. *Ran.* It pained my stiff knee, but I didn't care. Up the hummock past the oil shed. Words drummed through my mind in time to my footbeats: *Please don't tell about Wah Chung. Please don't tell about Wah Chung.*

Papa looked up quick when I entered. "Amos and Mr. Tyler are here," I said. Then the drumbeat words: "Please don't tell about Wah Chung!"

He didn't reply, but set his mouth hard and brushed past me out the door.

He was walking so fast I had to run to catch up. "Please," I said, tugging at his sleeve. "Please don't tell." He yanked his arm, shook me off. Wouldn't even look at me. "Papa, he did nothing amiss. And Dr. Wilton said he'd see to him, if it's right by you. Please, won't you just say he's gone?"

Papa stopped, turned to face me. "I don't hold with lying, Eliza Jane. Nor with liars."

I sagged backward, stung by the anger in his voice, by the disappointment in his eyes. A liar. That was what he thought of me.

But I *had* lied.

As we rounded the oil shed I saw Mr. Tyler and Amos coming toward us. Not Mama. She'd likely stayed in the house with Wah Chung.

Mr. Tyler shook Papa's hand. "Keeper," he said.

Papa said, "Henry. Amos. What brings you here?"

"I'll come straight to the nub of it. Amos says you got a Chinaman hid out here on the island. Do you know of any such?"

Papa nodded. "I do. A boy—and he's not hiding. We've let him in the house for now."

"In your house? After *that?*" Mr. Tyler slewed his gaze at me. My hand flew up to finger the bruise beneath my eye.

"*He* didn't do it!" I turned to glare at Amos. Is *that* what he'd said? I thought to pin the blame back where it belonged, on Amos, but stopped myself. "It was . . . a mishap," I said. The truth.

Amos's face flamed; he leaned down to flick a lump of mud off the toe of his boot. Papa looked, frowning, from Amos to me and back again at Amos.

"I've spoke to some folks on the committee," Mr. Tyler said. "They want you to give him over to us."

Papa hesitated. "I can set him on a ship for San Francisco," he said mildly. "Save you a heap of trouble."

"No. We aim to . . . show him around town some first. A lesson, like, to any others might be lurking hereabouts."

"He wasn't lurking!" I flashed out. "He didn't have anywhere to go."

"Eliza, leave us *now!* Go to the house this instant."

I moved in that direction—but slowly—and stopped just around the corner.

"Amos says *you* didn't know the Chinaman was hid in your shed," I heard Mr. Tyler say. "And takin' him in for the storm—that was only decent. But if I ain't mistook, that inspector don't like you keepin' strangers on lighthouse land, without you got his say-so. Now, if you give him over to us, no one can fault you for what's done. But if you keep him here for no good cause . . . well, that's a horse of a different breed."

"Is that a threat, Henry?" Something hard in Papa's voice.

"No call for threats. Just give over the Chinaman to me."

I peered around the house, saw Papa draw in

a long breath. He seemed to gaze *through* Mr. Tyler and Amos, and out to sea. For a moment hope swelled within me. He wouldn't give up Wah Chung. He would fetch him to Dr. Wilton and explain to the inspector that he couldn't have done other than take him in during the storm. Then, "He's but a boy," Papa said. "You'll do him no harm? I have your word on it?"

"We ain't harmed a hair on their heads. That ain't our way."

"Not harmed?" The words blurted out of me; I couldn't stop them. "Dragging them out of their very homes? Shoving them into those carts? Scaring them half to death? That's doing no harm?"

"Eliza, get in the house this minute!" Papa's eyes spat sparks.

"If you give him to them, you're a hypocrite, Papa. A pharisee. You'll be going against what it says in your very own Bible!"

"My Bible says, 'Blessed is the man that walketh not in the counsel of the ungodly, nor standeth in the way of sinners,'" Papa growled.

"'For I was an hungred, and ye gave me meat: I was thirsty, and ye gave me drink: I was a stranger, and ye took me in.'" I was shouting now. Amos gaped at me. Mr. Tyler stared like I was Satan himself, then turned to look at Papa like he expected him to take me in hand. But Papa stood speechless—whether from anger or shock or mortification, I couldn't say. I felt ashamed, seeing myself through his eyes. I was wayward and shrill—as far from a lady as it is possible to be. I thought, for a moment, of sparing Papa the rest of it. I wasn't blurting now. I *could* stop, if I chose. And yet it seemed to me that there was a time for being a lady, and a time for laying truth out on the air.

"And Jesus said, 'Inasmuch as ye have done it unto one of the least of these my brethren, ye have done it unto me.' And to the folks who *didn't* give aid he said the same thing, Papa— that whatever kindness they withheld from the least of his brethren, they withheld it from him."

"'Honor thy father and thy mother!'" Papa bellowed out. He glowered at me for a long moment, then turned again toward the sea. He looked . . . weary. And I began to feel bad, using Papa's own Bible against him when I wasn't even certain how much of it *I* believed. I began to feel . . . unkind.

"Leave it be, James, don't be a fool," Mr.

Tyler said. "We'll fetch the boy out. It won't lay on your conscience."

Papa didn't move. His eyes searched the horizon, like he hoped for something clear and certain to sail into view.

"That inspector won't fault you for what you done if you give him to us now. If not . . ."

Slowly Papa turned to me. "There is a steep price to be paid for this, Eliza. Think on it."

Seemed like he was asking *me* for some way out. Asking me for . . . dispensation, so he could stave off another *blot* and still stand tall in my eyes. I recollected something Mama had said, that Papa was not as strong as he appeared.

Someway, I had thought that he could put all to rights. That no matter how many blots there were, we wouldn't truly have to leave. He wouldn't allow it to happen. But now . . . *A steep price*. Seemed like this *might* spell the end.

I looked about the island and felt such a pang in my heart. Never again to watch harbor seal pups at play or whales scratching off barnacles against these shoals. Never again to breathe this clean salt air or to walk between parted waters across the seafloor.

And a cowardly voice inside me was saying,

They won't truly harm Wah Chung. To give up all for him now would be foolish. They'll parade him through town, then ship him to San Francisco. He can tolerate that.

But powerful words were still in my mouth; I let them come.

"It would taint us, Papa. We would never be the same."

17

LAST LOOK BACK

The doctor came. It was not long after Amos and his father had left; likely they had passed on the isthmus.

He and Papa spoke alone in the tower for a spell. They summoned Wah Chung; when he came down, he told me that Papa would take him away that night, but he wouldn't tell me where to. Nor would Dr. Wilton, who left shortly after with only a nod for Mama and me.

Presently Mr. Pemberton arrived, a rifle slung over his shoulder. He and Papa strode down to the isthmus, sat on the bench by the path. I worried the whole while. What would happen if Mr. Tyler roused up that rabble and led them here?

Mama and Wah Chung and I set back to work. When Mama went upstairs for a moment, Wah Chung took me aside. "There is spirit here," he said. "In you house. Baby, I think."

I gaped at him. "*Spirit?*"

He nodded. "Spirit. Ghost. You fetch bones home, across water. Spirit rest."

Ghost. That set my spine to tingling. I recalled the crying I'd heard that night, after the baby died. It had seemed so real. . . .

At last the sea sealed off the way to the island, and we were safe until the nighttime ebb. When it came, I bade Wah Chung farewell.

Nothing private could be said there in the sitting room, in front of Papa and Mama and Mr. Pemberton. "Very please know you," Wah Chung said. I nodded. I knew I should say something, but I couldn't scrape the words loose from my throat.

At the last moment, just as Wah Chung was turning away, I said, "Wait. Please." I ran up to my room, picked up a sea-polished agate, a sand dollar, and a striped shell, then ran back down again. "For you," I said.

Wah Chung took them, looking dismayed. "I have . . . nothing give *you*," he said.

"But you've already given me . . ." I glanced at Papa. "Just take them. Please."

He did.

After they left, I climbed the stairs again—all the way to the lantern room, where Mama tended the light. The beacon picked them out as they crossed the isthmus—Papa with his long-legged stride, Wah Chung half running behind. They climbed up the mountain of logs and driftwood left by the storm and then, near the top of it, Papa stopped and turned back. Wah Chung caught up to him; they seemed to converse there for a moment. Then they turned north, away from the harbor, crested the driftwood heap together, and vanished into the dark.

Hope is a hardy plant, tougher than blackberry bushes, I think. In spite of Mr. Tyler's threats to notify the Lighthouse Service, in spite of the blot on Papa's record, I could not conceive of leaving.

Still, during the dozen or so days we waited, we began setting our affairs in order. Mama finished the pillow she'd been embroidering for the settee. She planted some bulbs on either side of the front stoop. "Windflowers," she said, kind of wistful. "I hope they will *like* wind."

Papa put the last coat of varnish on the redwood table he had carved and set it beneath the banjo clock. He asked Mr. Pemberton to help him move the marble ballast stone a sea captain had given him the previous spring. They set it into a mound of earth near the front door, as a bench of sorts. Sometimes, when I looked up into the tower room, I saw Papa staring—just staring—out to sea. He wouldn't tell where he had taken Wah Chung. But he never punished me for harboring him. His anger seemed to have scattered on the wind; when he spoke to me now, he seemed somewhere far away.

Sadie cried when I told her we might have to go. I never thought she'd cry. "You can't leave," she said. "You *can't.*"

My heart was so sore! I didn't think that I could bear it.

Once, coming down for a glass of water late at night, I heard Mama and Papa talking in the sitting room. "Surely he won't punish you for this, James," Mama said. "You couldn't have put that boy out in the storm. And Henry Tyler had no right to him. You got him off the island soon enough."

"Even if he finds no fault with my actions, he'll see I can't control my daughter. On a light station . . . that could be enough."

Well. No water that night. Only tears.

Often when I came home from school, there were ladies in the sitting room, come to call on Mama. Not everyone came. Some folks shunned us, hearing we'd refused to turn over Wah Chung. This hurt Mama, I could tell, but she put on a good front. "And they call themselves *ladies*," she sniffed when Mrs. Cuthbertson and Mrs. Somersby made a spectacle of moving away from us at church.

Papa . . . Well. He sat brooding and grim.

Dr. Wilton gave me a magnifying glass when I came to talk to him about the favor I had to ask. The glass was heavy—brass rimmed, with a thick lens. "That secret world of yours is everywhere," he said. "No matter where you go."

He granted the favor. Two days later Papa crossed the isthmus carrying a small wooden box. "We'll bury her here, on the island," he said, setting down the sad little coffin on our front stoop. *You fetch bones home.*

Mama burst into tears; Papa put his arms around her. "She belongs *here*, Rose. The doctor persuaded me of that. No matter what becomes of us, she'll be here." Papa brushed the tears from her cheeks, then drew back and pulled something from his inside coat pocket. Three tiny evergreen seedlings. "California cypress," Papa said. He was eyeing me oddly. "Amos gave me these when I was coming back from town. He said they were for you."

Amos! I recollected how he had looked when I hadn't told his father *all* about my bruise. I lifted the seedlings to my nose, breathed in the freshness of them. Were they intended as a bribe? I wondered. So I wouldn't tell? Or maybe . . . as payback because I hadn't?

Papa dug the grave, and I planted the three seedlings, wide spaced, about it. After, in the drizzling rain, we held a little service. Mama and I picked wildflowers; Papa read a passage from the Bible:

"'I returned, and saw under the sun, that the race is not to the swift, nor the battle to the strong, neither yet bread to the wise, nor yet riches to men of understanding, nor yet favor to men of skill; but time and chance happeneth to them all.'"

Time and chance happeneth to them all.

There was such a letting go in that passage! The words, when Papa said them, sounded wise and deep. And yet it seemed to me that what they meant was: *Life is not fair. There is no protection.* Purely counter to the passages Papa generally read, passages about God's justice. Punishment for sins. Virtue rewarded.

So the very Bible owned up to it: even the Shepherd couldn't protect.

And yet . . .

Something happened that night that I still can't explain. I haven't told anyone before now; I couldn't. They'd think I was dreaming—or dotty. Maybe it was a dream, though it didn't seem so then.

I sat up in bed feeling pricklish, as if someone were watching me sleep. I looked about the room. No one there.

"Mama?"

I pulled on my shawl, tiptoed to her door. Snoring—Papa. And the little clicking breath sounds Mama makes.

The light that seeped down from the tower was specially bright. I felt drawn toward it someway. *Led.* I climbed the stairs.

A thick fog had rolled in. It held the beacon glow, pressed it back into the tower, as fog was wont to do. The lens seemed hewn from frozen light; the little room was pulsing.

Here is the peculiar thing. The light just kept coming. It spilled in through the windows, trickled through the openings in the floor. It sifted like blown sand through the caulking between metal and glass. It flurried, fine and powdery, through the solid iron roof, as if some threshold had been crossed.

Light.

I was flooded with light. It pressed against my eyes and tingled in my skin. It glimmered beneath my fingernails, sizzled in my hair.

All at once something bright and hot went shuddering through me, and I felt such a rushing in, such a flowing out, of love. For Mama and Papa. For Sadie and Wah Chung. For Dr. and Mrs. Wilton. For my baby sister, who couldn't cross to this world alive. For the beauty of this place—from the whole huge beauty of the sky down to the beauty of the smallest starfish under the waves. Down to the beauty in a sprinkling of sand, in the cells of a drop of blood.

And why, I wondered then—if the world were but a cold and chancy and godless place—why would it possess such an extravagance of beauty, such an overflow of love?

When the inspector came, that hardy plant, hope, stretched sunward and waved its leaves. One more chance, I kept thinking. He'll give us one more chance.

He and Papa stayed upstairs for more than an hour. When they came down again, neither one would meet our eyes. Mama started to offer a slice of pie but, seeing their faces, stopped.

This time Papa didn't walk with the inspector across the isthmus, but only spoke with him for a spell on the front stoop. When he came into the house, his face looked slack and wounded. Something in his eyes had gone soft.

"It's a shore commission," he said. "A desk job. Clerking. Far from the sea."

The last time the waters parted for us, a warm June breeze blew in from the southwest. The perfume of wildflowers was strong in the air and mingled with the smell of the sea. We trudged back and forth with our belongings, packing them into Mr. Hinkley's cart on the mainland. Parthenia we tethered behind. She bleated, sorrowful, like she knew she'd never return.

I tried to gather up the whole look and smell

and sound and feel of our lost home and lock it in a safe place where it would never slip from memory. And yet even then I couldn't compass all of it. Even then it had begun to fade.

On our final crossing, just as I reached shore, I heard a stirring in the air behind me. I looked back to see seven brown pelicans lumbering in single file across the sky—as if they were performing some ancient rite. They dipped down, swooped one by one right *beside* the keeper's walk. A salute, I thought. A farewell. Then they were pumping their wings, rising in a lazy, graceful arc, sweeping away to the north.

My heart swelled with aching, took up all the space in my chest.

I wondered if Moses had felt so when he walked across the Red Sea and struck out for an unknown land. But no. This was not what Moses had done. This was not moving *toward* something promised. It was leaving—like Adam and Eve—taking a long, last look back at Eden.

October 1888
Brecksville, Ohio

ANDREW JOHN

I have some sand in my left knee, and it's mighty curious to look upon. Mama *tried* to wash it out, but that was tricksome right then. She stanched the wound with cornstarch. I should have had a stitch. Still, I'm partial to that sand. A piece of the island where we used to live, now part of me forever.

Look there, Andrew John, on the wall. It's the island I was speaking of. That painting came some weeks past, sent to the new keeper, then here to us by post. I looked for a letter, but there was none.

Still, I know who made it. A friend of mine. Wah Chung.

Some days I yearn to know what became of him.

Most days that painting makes me sad.

There is sadness in our family, Andrew John. You'll see that, when you're able. A body can do what she knows is right and still bring sorrow to the ones she loves.

Papa didn't take to clerking. He doesn't take much to farming, but that is what he does, on the land his father left. Some days Papa's sadness wraps about us like a cloak.

But even so . . .

I had thought, when we first left California, that there would be nothing much worth seeing someplace else. That my larking days were done. After the island. After the lighthouse. After the sea.

But here there are tadpoles in the spring. They sprout tiny, perfect legs and turn into frogs—pea-sized!—in summer. They tickle when you hold them. There is ice on the crick in winter. When you get down on your hands and knees, you can see fish squiggling by underneath. And in the magnifying glass there is a whole secret world: snowflakes like tatted doilies, fantastical creatures in a drop of pond water, jungles in a patch of moss.

There are astonishing things in this world, Andrew John. And beyond what we can see are things more astonishing still.

Then there's you. The doctor told Mama she would have no more babies, and yet here you are—three weeks old—with your pink feet waving in the air, with your smile like to light up the world.

On clear nights, when you're older, we'll take you up stargazing. Papa will tote the telescope; Mama and I will fetch cake and lemonade. We'll head for the knoll behind the orchard.

Papa has charts. He knows every constellation—every star, I think. He takes comfort in the certainty of stars—that each one moves in its appointed round, night after night after night.

But the names of constellations blur together in my mind. I can't recollect them. When I look at stars, I like to wonder. About a fire so hot it would melt the very ground beneath your feet. About a space so vast we're like dust specks on its boots. About spinning on a roundish rock through a heaven of flame and ice—and we scarcely even know it. And I wonder: What worlds would we see if we had sharper lenses? And what worlds beyond those worlds?

We're living in a place where there is mystery all around. Mystery inside, in the cells of our blood; mystery outside, in the stars. Mystery before we're born; mystery after we die. Mystery so deep, it busts clean out of the charts we try to pen it in.

Terrible things can happen in this world—things you can't explain away. It's not safe here, Andrew John. I can't promise you'll be safe.

But there are miracles, too—like you. And love. And glories well beyond our knowing.

AUTHOR'S NOTE

This book, like all historical novels, is a hybrid of history and imagination. I will try to shed light on the boundaries—where one leaves off and the other begins.

In the latter years of the nineteenth century many virulent racist attacks were carried out against the Chinese in this country. In Los Angeles in 1871 a mob shot, hanged, and stabbed nineteen Chinese to death. In 1880 rioters rampaged through Denver's Chinese quarters, injuring many and killing one. In Rock Springs, Wyoming, a band of armed miners attacked their Chinese coworkers, killing twenty-eight men and chasing several hundred from their homes and mining claims. The Chinese community in Seattle was burned down in 1885. That same year, mobs expelled the Chinese communities from Tacoma, Washington, as well as from smaller towns in six Washington counties.

In Eureka, California, in February of 1885, after a Chinese man accidentally shot a white city councilman, the entire community of Chinese in that city were forced out of their homes and shipped to San Francisco. This event seems to have galvanized the fears and prejudices against the Chinese in Crescent City, just up the coast.

Although there is no doubt that the Chinese community was expelled from Crescent City, the timing of the expulsion is in question. While some writers have put the date in 1885, this seems unlikely in light of other evidence. A 1954 article in the *Del Norte Triplicate* quotes from 1886 issues of the old *Del Norte Record*. In March of 1886, the *Record* later said, an article by its editor "marked the beginning of the death blow for the Chinamen in the county." By April 24 the *Record* claimed that the 177 Chinese formerly in Del Norte County had been reduced to "between three and seven." However, all issues of that newspaper published in 1885 and 1886 have since been lost.

The Del Norte County Historical Society's records contain two detailed accounts of the expulsion written by the same man, Joseph F. Endert, who witnessed the event when he was eight years old. One account, published in the *Bulletin of the Del Norte County Historical Society*, sets the date early in 1886. The other account, quoted in the *Triplicate*, cites June 19 of the same year.

We may never know for certain precisely when the event occurred. I have relied heavily upon Joseph Endert's account of what happened, including the ringing of the dinner bell; the men with clubs threatening the sheriff; the loading of Chinese women, children, and two old men into carts; the transporting of them to Edwards Corner; and the shipping to San Francisco. I have set the date somewhere between the two he cites, which makes it roughly consistent with the dates set forth in the quoted pieces from the *Del Norte Record*.

Meanwhile, the California Newspaper Project, which seeks to put on microfilm every newspaper ever published in California, continues to search for the lost issues of the *Del Norte Record*. Should those issues ever come to light, we may after all find out exactly when the expulsion actually occurred.

The Crescent City lighthouse, now known as Battery Point, is real. I have described it in the book as accurately as I can—down to the pump organ, the redwood table, the ballast-stone bench, the California cypress trees, and the banjo clock. In 1886 the lens was a magnificent fourth-order Fresnel, designed in France by the famous lens maker Augustin-Jean Fresnel. The lighthouse is a museum now, open to the public (when tides permit) during the spring and summer months. But the beacon still shines every night of the year, as a private aid to navigation.

Although there was a family living in the lighthouse

in 1886—the family of Captain John Jeffrey lived there from 1875 to 1914—the family in my book is entirely fictional and not in the least bit based upon the Jeffreys. In fact, with the exception of Sheriff Endert (Joseph Endert's father), the Ahrens boy (who was mentioned in one of Joseph Endert's eyewitness accounts as Horace Ahrens in the other as Albert Ahrens), and Mrs. Overmeyer (whose dinner bell is likewise mentioned), all of the characters in this book are completely fictional.

I did borrow one true incident, which occurred in the lighthouse during Captain Jeffrey's tenure. During one particularly fierce storm a wave knocked off the cookstove chimney, setting fire to the kitchen. Soon after, another wave washed over the kitchen and down the chimney hole, putting out the fire. The kitchen was destroyed beyond repair.

Perusing the files of the Del Norte County Historical Society, I found several accounts of a young Chinese boy who was sent at the time of the expulsion to a farm on the Winchuck River in Oregon. My parents, as it happens, lived until recently on thirteen acres of former farmland on the Winchuck. I like to think of Wah Chung there, eating well and resting up—as I used to do when I visited—before finding his way south to San Francisco.

ACKNOWLEDGMENTS

This book would not have been possible without the generous help of so many people! Ruthanne Lum McCunn read the manuscript twice and gave me reliable, sensitive feedback and many excellent suggestions. Her own books, *Thousand Pieces of Gold* and *Wooden Fish Songs*, were so illuminating! Dr. Leslie Hulton vetted the manuscript, then took time to go to a medical library to look up medical practices and nomenclature of the historical period in question. I have received help from three sets of keepers of Battery Point Lighthouse. Nadine and Jerry Tugel showed me the lighthouse and answered many questions. Nadine also vetted the manuscript, and her own publications on the topic were invaluable. Nancy and Larry Schnider generously hosted me overnight at the lighthouse, fed me breakfast, answered more questions, and went digging for obscure facts on my behalf. Don and Carol Vestal spent an afternoon sharing yet more information with me.

Ron Severson of Lakeridge High School gave me fascinating perspectives on biology, taught me how to use a microscope, and lent me some of his slides. Matt Bozulich of Portland State University also took time to show me what Eliza might see through a microscope's lens. The staff of the Del Norte County Historical Society guided me through their treasure trove of materials and copied the information I needed. Cheryl Hatswell guided me to pertinent facts at the Oregon Historical Society, and Mary Norman, Margaret Zeps, Carole Dickerson, and the entire staff of the Lake Oswego Library spent untold hours digging for arcane information and providing moral support. Andrea Vanek of the California Newspaper Project searched for lost issues of Crescent City newspapers and told me exactly which issues were available and which had been lost. John Pritchett of *The Daily Triplicate* in Crescent City searched his archives for the same. Eileen Flory at the Oregon Coast Aquarium answered questions and sent me materials about coastal fauna. Christina Palm lent me her paper on the Chinese immigrants in the West, which gave me an excellent overview. Pat Flitcroft read the manuscript and gave me an insider's view of what it's like to grow up in a lighthouse. Becky Huntting proofread the manuscript and aided in my understanding of spiritual matters. My agent, Emilie Jacobson, gave me enthusiastic support. Pamela Smith Hill read the entire manuscript and gave me excellent suggestions. Winifred Morris provided an invaluable firsthand perspective on goat ownership, and Dorothy Morrison lent me two antique books on everyday life in these times. And my entire evening critique group—Winnie and Dorothy, as well as Margaret Bechard, Ellen Howard, David Gifaldi, Eric Kimmel, Rebecca Hickox, and Robin Cody—gave me help, inspiration, and confidence throughout the project.

Thank you, one and all!

Finally, I'd like to express appreciation for my editors on this project. Jean Karl was my first editor; as ever, she encouraged me to dig deep and find the book I was reaching for. I will always be profoundly grateful for having had the opportunity to work with her on this and five other books. Jon Lanman's perceptive editing helped me to bring this one home, with additional help and support from Ginee Seo and Brenda Bowen.